THE ECHO 1

COLD
BETWEEN
STARS

BELINDA CRAWFORD

HENDRIX & FAUST
PUBLISHERS

Published by Hendrix & Faust, Publishers in 2020

Text copyright © Belinda Crawford 2020

www.belindacrawford.com

ISBN: 978-0-6484881-4-9 (ebook)
ISBN: 978-0-6484881-5-6 (paperback)

A catalogue record for this book is available from the National Library of Australia

GLOSSARY

SPECIES

Jøran (a.k.a. the kin)
The overarching name for the three species
native to Jørn, which are:

Qwan (air-kin): Avians with four eyes and two sets of wings.

Rucnart (tree-kin): Gigantic felines with four eyes and six legs.

Swatai (water-kin): Small, lizard-like amphibians.

Jørgen
A Human—Jøran hybrid.

PSIONICS

Psion
Someone with the ability to read and/or influence the emotions
and/or thoughts of others (a.k.a. an empath or telepath).

Aer
A telepathic dream world constructed by the kin.

Eter
The mental space within an individual's mind, from which they can
construct their own reality and engage with other psions.

Anima
The core of a person, also known as their spirit or soul.

CHAPTER ONE

You don't dream in stasis/sleep, not really. I mean, Mum does. And Dad and Jim Engineer and Mae Lu Medic, and, really, all the older humans. And, well, I guess some of my friends dream too, but only the mostly human ones.

And Mac, but Mac's weird.

So, yeah, some of us don't dream in stasis/sleep. I mean, we catch a few REM cycles every now and then because otherwise it's like a one-way shuttle to the Crazy System. But, yeah, we don't dream.

We don't really sleep either. Not a regular kind of sleep, where your head touches your pillow and then, *BAM*, it's morning already and your dad's got your ankles and he's dragging you out of bed because you slept through the alarm and it's your turn to muck out the cyclers.

Not that kind of sleep. For one, there's goo up my nose and in my ears and down my throat. It'd be kinda gross except if tastes like tao-quice – sweet and smooth and warm, like sunshine, or how I imagine it must feel; and smells like Mae Lu's pancakes – butter curling up my nose and fresh cut mawberries tingling on my tongue. And it's warm and soft and, honestly, most of the time I don't feel it or taste it or smell it because, most of the time, I'm in my head. Or, more accurately, other people's heads.

Like now.

I hadn't meant to slip into Mum's, or any other dreamer's head. Dreamers are boring and freaky and Off Limits – Onah says it like that, with the capitals, as if those two letters make the words magical or something; but Mum's pod is right next to mine and she's having one of her bad cycles. Normally I can shut her out, but this one's really bad. Like super-mega-force bad. If she'd been in normal sleep, she'd have jerked herself out of it by now, but stasis/sleep's got her stuck and her fear is lashing at me – thick, black ropes of it tangling in my head and curling in my chest.

Before I know it, those ropes have pierced my heart and grown sharp, sticky thorns and, Old Terra, it hurts, hurts like you wouldn't believe. Hurts like a shard of acid slowly melting my heart, and then *YANK*, I'm in Mum's dream.

I'm not supposed to be able to see what she dreams. I'm an empath and I should only be able to sense her emotions, but Mum's got a hint of telepathy somewhere in her DNA, and well, she's my mum. Some rules don't apply.

I really wish this one did though because there's some shit you don't need to see. And right now, I don't need to see Mum naked with vines wrapped around her body, her eyes bugging out of her head and her mouth wide open as she screams. The sound goes all the way through my eardrums, a shard of steelglas slicing up my brain, my throat, my chest. I want to cover my ears, except I can't. My arms are held at my sides, like Mum's, bound in the same oily green vines – thick and fleshy.

They squeeze tighter and tighter, winding up my chest so tight the skin bulges in the gaps between in little, fleshy mountains. Somehow, I'm naked now too and the vines are sliding around me, rippling like long, boneless fingers, squidgy and clammy as they climb higher. My ribs grind together. My heart thumps. It's hard to breathe.

Red. Red so bright it rivals a star, bursts in my face. Wet and hot, it drips down my nose, trickles over my lips, down my chin. Then. Pain. Burning, searing. I look down. There are thorns growing out of my chest, huge bony things, glowing red-hot, the flesh – my flesh – around them ripped, bloody and already sizzling.

It – no, *me* – I smell like cooking wombacow. The meaty, fatty stench razes my nose, spikes in my brain, grows a few friends and rips open my skull—

Ķuma.

—before it dives for my stomach, bringing up breakfast and lunch and an endless torrent of sweet, warm goo—

Kuma.

The voice doesn't belong to this dream. It's not even really a voice, just a presence; a clear, sparkling white surrounding a boiling core of black. *Kuma*, it says again. *Out.*

And *WHACK*, I'm back in my own head, my own sane, non-dreaming head. I can still sense Mum, can sense those sticky black tendrils of fear reaching for me, trying to suck me back in, but the white/black presence is a plasteel wall between us. The tendrils smack and writhe against it, but the presence, Onah's presence, doesn't so much as twitch.

Safe.

Relief swamps me from head to toe even as guilt knots in my chest. I'm safe from Mum's nightmare but she's still caught. Perhaps, with Onah still protecting me, I could reach in and—

WHOMP.

Ow.

No. It's less a word than a collection of images and emotions. A shaken head, a firm grip on the back of my neck, the hard blue/red stare of a four-eyed bird – Onah's stare – and a reprimand all in one. Onah doesn't say a lot, but he sure packs it in when he does. *The Dreamers are—*

Off Limits. I know, but—

Kuma. My name is a packet of memories and emotions coloured by the white/black of Onah's mind. A boy with golden skin and dark hair intent on the progress of ants. The same boy hiding from rucnarts, using his empathy to get his sister in trouble, to stop a fight then to start one. Frustration, patience, determination. Fear.

Fear. Of me? *Onah?*

Not you. Listen. See, Onah says.

Onah isn't human, I'm putting that out there because these things can get confusing and because, when he says 'listen and see', he's not talking about ears and eyes.

I spread my mind. There's no other word for how I open my brain and push myself outwards. It's a flood at first, like my shields are a dam that can barely hold me in, and the moment I let them go – *WHOOSH.* The whoosh is easy, a heady rush with my heart pounding, my fingers tingling and a 'whoop' ripping from my throat. It's the rest that's hard.

Soon enough the wave slows, thins, and the rush becomes a trickle wrapping around spots of colour, like pebbles in a stream that I can touch. Some are coals – burning spots in the palm of my mind; some are chips of ice and others fizz against my brain, little itchy spots that jump and jiggle. Mum is one of those spots, a puke-yellow ball writhing behind my ear, wrapped in Onah's white/black sparkle. And there's Dad next to her, a cool glittery blue, and Jim Engineer beyond him, and Mae Lu and Mac and scores of others – human, mostly human and not human at all – that make the *Citlali* home. One-hundred and eighty-nine shifting, coloured pebbles brushing against my mind. It all seems as it should, except…

Why was everything so still?

Something's wrong. I imbue 'wrong' with the stillness and the silence that's crawling up my neck, that makes my stomach tight and my skin jittery.

The Dreamers are sick, Onah says. Sick. The word is grey-green, a vibration that tangles in my throat and grates down my spine. It feels like the vines in Mum's nightmare, wrapping around my ankles, the thorns ripping through my chest, the searing smell of meat.

I see it then. The thin, almost translucent veins of sickness snaking between the Dreamers. They pulse and shiver, alive and yet not. I touch one, a light brush with my mind. It bites, a sharp sting that numbs my brain before I jerk away, but in that short contact I see the Dreamers, connected one to the other.

Just the Dreamers. Only the Dreamers.

It takes a second for that to sink in.

I dive back in, forcing my mind into all of the *Citlali's* nooks and crannies, seeking, searching. There are one-hundred and eighty-nine coloured pebbles in my mind, but of the restless coils of energy, of those of us who are only part human, the ones who don't dream, there is nothing.

Where's Grea? An image of a girl who looks like me, same dark hair and gold skin, same dark eyes, arms crossed and sneering at me from the other side of the room.

You have to wake.

I am awake.

No, you have to wake.

An image of the stasis pod's dome, of my hand reaching out and touching the warm plasglas. My fingers contorting to fit the emergency release.

But— My heart squeezes, panic riding it hard. We're only halfway through the cycle. If I open my pod now... *It's not time.*

Wake. Onah pinning a chick with all four eyes, the weight of them bearing down, down, down until the chick crumples into a little, fluff-covered ball.

I push back and somewhere behind the weight of Onah's command, I sense a tight, white/black ball of panic and in it, around it, veins of sticky grey-green.

Onah bats me out.

You're sick.

WAKE. Onah – not his voice or his presence, but him, white around a boiling darkness – blasts through my mind. He burns through my bones, filling my skin and pushing me aside as he flows down my arm and takes hold of my hand. He presses it against the stasis pod's dome and holds it there until the 'glas flashes red.

Once, twice, three times.

And then Onah's gone, the goo's being ripped out of my throat and the pod's flashing and hissing and then... and then...

CHAPTER TWO

My knees hit the deck, then my hands. The sound rings in my ears and the cold cuts right through my skin and into my bones. The lights are so bright they're burning my eyes, but I don't care. I don't care, I don't care.

I can't breathe. Old Terra, I can't breathe. My mouth is open and I'm trying to suck in air, but my lungs feel like they're glued together and all I can do is make this thin, wheezy 'whuuuuuuuu'.

The light gets brighter, but I'm struggling so hard to breathe I can't close my eyes, and then I'm staring at a pair of human-shaped feet. Pale blue and bare. I can see right through them.

'Kuma Darzi, are you well?'

I gasp another lungful of air. 'Whuuuuuu.'

'Kuma Darzi?' The feet disappear and a second later I'm staring at a disembodied head floating above the floor. It's blue and round and soft, with great big eyes and short spiky hair, and like the feet I can see right through it. 'Breathe, Kuma.' The *Citlali's* avatar inhales, her nose scrunching, before she exhales, the air leaving her open mouth in a rush.

I copy it. The first breath is another thin, wheezy gasp but the second is better and my lungs are expanding. But it hurts, Old Terra, it hurts. The air is acid in my lungs – burning, melting – and I don't want to take a third but my chest is already expanding and in it pours, ripping away my insides even as I gulp another breath.

'Good.' The AI nods. 'There is still stasis gel in your lungs. Once it dissolves you will find it easier to breathe.'

'Hurts.' It's more a splutter than a word, spit and stasis gel flying from my lips. Coming out of stasis never hurt this much before, never felt like I was freezing and burning all at once. Never felt like I was dying.

'Your biology is readjusting to the ship's atmosphere. The pain will subside once the process is complete. For now, concentrate on breathing.'

I concentrate, but with each breath the mechanics of pushing my ribs out and squeezing them back in take less and less of my thoughts, leaving room for other things to intrude. Like the steelcrete under my hands, warmer than it was a few breaths ago, and the brush of air against my skin. My naked skin.

Shit.

My eyes catch on Citlali.

The avatar stares back.

I scramble to my feet and lunge for the wall panel opposite my pod. The panel has retracted before my fingers reach it, and instead of shiny off-white plasteel, I clutch at nano-cloth. Blessed nano-cloth, warm and smooth, already humming against my skin. My heart slows a beat then resumes its gallop as I shove arms and legs into the shipsuit. It's on in three seconds flat, and I run my hands down the front as it conforms to my body, lengthening here, shortening there, the colour changing from white to the pink camo I'd adopted before stasis.

'You appear to be recovered, Kuma Darzi.'

'Yeah—' My stomach clenches, and the cough that hacks its way out of my lungs leaves a thick, toa-quice flavoured ball of goo in its wake.

It's soft and squidgy on my tongue and I want to be sick, instead I spit it out where it splots on the deck – a golden ball of mucus that slowly glides toward my toes.

I scuttle back before a trio of blue, fuzzy critters skitter over my feet and converge on what I can only guess was the last of the stasis gel taking up residence in my lungs. I turn away before they start cleaning up. Normally I like watching them work, but right now, watching mammals the size of my thumb fight over the stuff I hacked out of my lungs is pushing it.

There aren't many places to look in the stasis unit, just the shiny bulkhead hiding our clothes, Mum, Dad, my sister and my empty pod.

The rest of my family is sleeping, floating in stasis gel. Why aren't they awake?

And then I remember the vines wrapping through Mum's nightmare and the sickness winding through the Dreamers. My forehead tingles at the memory of its bite.

'Kuma Darzi, are you well?'

'I— Ah, um, yeah I guess.'

The avatar cocked her head. 'You pressed the emergency release.' She tilted her head the other way. 'Why?'

'I didn't. That was Onah. He said there was something wrong with the Dreamers.'

There is a moment, as I tell her about Onah pushing the release button, where the avatar flickers. Citiali is a new AI, but the whole psion thing is pretty new too, or at least it was when she left space dock. Every now and again she has trouble when you tell her things that defy the logic of physics (like Onah pushing a button in my pod when he was on the other side of the ship). It takes her an extra nanosecond to process the information. You'd have thought she'd have integrated it a little better some time during the hundred and twenty-three years we've been cruising around our corner of the galaxy, but no. Still takes an extra nanosecond.

But this time… this time the nanosecond is more like two, like her core is focussed elsewhere, which it probably is, since she controls an entire ship and all, but…

Yeah. *But.*

There's this creepy-crawly sensation in my belly that's got nothing to do with the memory of hacking up stasis gel and everything to do with the oily, grey-green vines wrapping around Mum's dreaming self.

Mum's stasis pod is right next to mine, the rounded plasglas clouded with condensation. I leave streaky handprints in the water as I wipe the droplets away. Inside, floating in the blue-green goo, Mum appears peaceful, no sign of the nightmare in her expression. There's maybe a little more grey in her otherwise black hair, but apart from that, she looks like she did when she snatched my biocomp away and closed the door on my stasis pod.

Still, that sickness is writhing around in my belly and now it's joined by this nagging sensation in the back of my head. 'Wake her up.' The words are out of my mouth before they form in my brain.

Citiali appears on the surface. Just her face, blotting out what I can see of Mum. 'I cannot,' she says.

'Sure you can.'

'No.'

'Why not?'

The avatar flickers and there's that pause again, those few nanoseconds that give the creepy-crawly feeling legs so that it can swallow my chest whole. 'I cannot, Kuma Darzi.'

'Okay.' I'm not quite sure if my lungs are working right or not, because it's getting a little hard to breathe. The creepy-crawlies aren't helping, taking up space behind my ribs that should be there for my lungs to go in and out. 'Okay,' I say again. 'I'll wake her up manually. I can do that.'

I'm pretty sure I can do that. Mai Lu makes sure to drill emergency procedures into the junior crew every chance she gets. It's just that I might have been doing something else when she did it last, and I might not have been paying attention to which buttons she pressed the time before that, or what she meant when she said we had to be really careful not to soak the gel.

I'm pretty sure it has something to do with the oxygen levels, but... Yeah, there's that *but* again.

Buts aren't going to get my mum out of stasis. I flex my fingers over the dome, warming them up like an Old Terra pianist, and touch the golden circle in the middle. Holos spring up around my hand: heart rate and blood oxygen and, I don't know, stuff that tells me Mum's alive and breathing in the blue-green goo. And there, at eye level, is the button that says "revive". My heart's beating hard, competing with the creepy-crawlies and my lungs for space in my chest. I flex my fingers again, trying to chase the nerves out. It doesn't work.

I press the button.

Nothing.

I press it again.

Still nothing.

There should be graphs and yellow words popping up in my face. I remember that much because Mai Lu screeched at me when she realised I wasn't paying attention. She'd used that particularly shrill tone that I swear can cut through bulkheads, and even now the memory of it makes my ears ache.

There aren't any graphs though, or Mai Lu to stand at my shoulder and yell in my ear. There's just the "Revive" button and Mum floating in the stasis pod, a thick sheet of plasglas and fifty litres of goo between me and her.

I hit the button, my fist driving right through the holo to smack against the pod. Apparently creepy-crawlies feed on frustration, or else there's something else growing my chest, shoving a lump up my throat.

The pod remains stubbornly closed.

'Citiali, why's it not working?'

Her face materialises under my fist. 'All systems are functioning normally.'

'No they're not. I can't wake Mum.'

There's a thread of desperation in my voice. It's born from the tightness in my chest, the mess of anxiety, frustration and the creepy-crawlies.

'Open it!'

'I cannot.'

I bang my fist on the pod. Through the holos and goo, Mum is peaceful. *And dead*, a small part of me says but I push it away. She's not dead, the monitors keeping track of her heart say so and I can sense her in my head, still gripped in the nightmare.

'Dad.' He bursts into my head like a revelation. That makes it sound like I forgot I have two parents, but I didn't. I'd been so fixated on Mum...

There are only four pods in the stasis unit, and Dad is right next to Mum. His pod is misted over with condensation as well, and I wipe it away to make sure he's in there. Dad's a tall man, with my pale gold skin and black hair, and he's hard to miss even amongst the gel. Like Mum, he appears serene, and maybe a little dead, but no, I can sense him too. Peaceful where Mum's freaking out in her nightmare.

Relief floods through me and I rest my head on the pod for a second, before I touch the revive button. His vitals spread over the plasglas, and... and...

No, that can't be right. It can't be.

The bouncing line that tracks Dad's heart is flat, like flatter than the decking. Next to it, the map of his brain is dark, no bright pops of colour showing his dreaming mind. Nothing.

'That's not possible.' My voice echoes in the stasis unit. I turn, seeking Citlali. She's back to hovering behind me, pale blue and transparent enough to glimpse the bulkhead through her. 'My dad's not dead.'

Citlali's expression turns confused for a second. 'Jiro Darzi died two weeks, three days and seventeen hours ago.'

'But he's not dead. I can *feel* him.'

And there's that flicker, a nanosecond too long as Citlali processes the concept of being able to feel someone without physically touching them.

When she finishes flickering, Citlali is wearing a sad, sympathetic expression. It's one of those slightly *wrong* expressions, where her eyes are a fraction too large and the corners of her mouth a little too downturned. Most of the time, Citlali is pretty good at simulating emotion, she's even funny on occasion, but she hasn't nailed the really big emotions yet, especially the grief and compassion she's trying to project now.

'I am sorry Kuma, but your parent is d—'

I interrupt her with a hand in her face. Like, *literally* in her face. The light particles that make up her form fizz and spit around my wrist.

'Citlali,' I say. 'You suck. Now, run a diagnostic.'

'All systems are operating within parameters.'

Frustration, anger and not a little fear boil out of my chest in a... let's not call it a scream. The sound echoes in the pod. 'Dad's not dead!'

'Jiro Darzi died two weeks—'

'Shut up!'

I'm breathing hard and my vision's kinda white around the edges, and there's this buzzing in my ears, drowning out the sound of the AI. It's like everything in the world is focussing down to the flat line on Dad's monitor, with its high-pitched whine somehow messing with the AI's words until all I hear is dead.

Dead.

Dead.

Not even the Dad-coloured whisper at the back of my psyche can drown it out, as if it says it often enough, maybe I'll believe it. And maybe I will because the AI can't be wrong. Can it? I mean, it's the ship.

Grea. Grea will know what to do.

There was one more pod to try and open. Grea. My twin sister's pod is right next to mine. The dome is almost white with condensation. I wipe it away, but there's still something clouding the plasglas, like the condensation somehow made it inside. I scrub harder, which is about as helpful as you would expect, and scowl at my reflection. Yeah, sometimes I'm not the brightest. Grea would argue that that was all the time, and then I'd send an *emote* into the nearest critter so strong, it would squeal and run up the nearest object, which was usually Grea's leg. And then she'd squeal and I'd smile and sometime later that night I'd find something nasty in my bed.

I hit the plasglas, trying to dislodge whatever it is clouding the inside of the pod.

A patch of… fug flakes away, leaving a hole big enough to peer through. I put my hand on the plasglas, spreading my fingers and leaning my forehead against it, squinting to see through the twilight inside the pod.

When I said twin before, I meant identical twin. My sister looks exactly like me, same black hair and gold skin, same dark eyes. Her hair is longer though, bound up in a braid that trails all the way down her back. You might ask how it happens that we're identical but not… what with me being a boy and Grea a girl. Well, for one, we're not *exactly* identical, and two, there are some things biology doesn't get right.

I can just make out Grea. Like Mum and Dad, she's floating in the stasis gel, eyes closed, but where they were peaceful, Grea's wearing a frown. No, not a frown but a full-on grimace – her face twisted up and teeth bared. She's curled on her side, knees to her chest, hugging them like she's trying to make herself really, really small.

Grea? I reach for her psionically, stretching through the goo with my mind, trying to connect with the part of my sister that's an empath like me. I stretch and stretch and stretch, further than I should have to, further even than when I searched the ship. Just like I did then, I sense nothing. My sister is right there in front of me, I shouldn't even have to reach for her.

She's my *twin*, my *identical* twin. We're not merely siblings, we're a whole, a living, functioning, interconnecting crazy-making whole. Even in stasis/sleep slipping into Grea's brain should be like talking to myself. It's not even like she's trying to shut me out, she's just not *there*.

A thought pops into my brain, not even fully formed, just a floating mass of emotion, like instinct and my heart stops in my chest.

Old Terra, what if she's dead?

Everything in me stops.

There's a big dark hole in the pit of my chest and I'm staring down its gullet.

What if she's dead?

No. No, she's not dead. She can't be dead. I saw her move, didn't I? Twitch her little finger?

Easier than breathing. Except breathing's not so easy at the moment. The creepy-crawlies are making a renewed assault on my chest and there's not enough oxygen in my lungs because my vision's going kinda dotty and there's that wheezing sound again as I try to draw in air.

The revive button is under my fingertips and Grea's vitals are spreading across the top, the lines and monitors moving like they should. Her heart jumping up and down in a steady rhythm, the neural monitor flashing with greens and reds. I frown at the picture of her brain. Is there meant to be that much red staining her cortex? The map makes it appear like there's a storm going on in my twin's head, popping and flashing with bursts of yellow and streaks of white.

A couple more thumps on the plasglas and more of the fug drops away, making a bigger window. I press my forehead to the pod once more, hands pressed flat either side of my head. It won't help me break through the... whatever the blank space is between us, but still...

Whatever it is, Grea's not dead. I won't let her be dead. I have to tell my heart that, and maybe my lungs, because right now it feels like the first is pounding the other flat against my ribs, squishing all the air out of my body.

It's so *quiet* in my head. I don't know how I didn't notice it before, maybe because I was too busy yelling at the AI. But now... now that quiet place is bringing back the pit in my chest and sucking all the warmth out of my bones. All I can see, all I can hear, is that silence and the endless black swallowing everything. Mum. Dad. Grea. The ship. Onah. The ship. The oxygen—

'Kuma?' Citlali is a blue glow in the corner of my vision. 'Remember to breathe, Kuma. In. Out.'

The memory of Citlali scrunching up her nose as she pretended to breathe flashes in front of my eyes, enough of a distraction to halt the spiral of panic.

And that's when I notice the fug clogging up Grea's pod, *really* notice it. One of the pieces I thumped loose is floating in front of my nose and it looks strange, like a piece of grey-green carpet trailing strands behind it. The strands wave and wriggle in the stasis gel, reaching out to similar strands on the fug still attached to the plasglas. They connect and the mired one kind of pulls the other back into place.

I jerk back. Stare at the door a second as the fug slides back over the clear patches. I turn to the Citlali. Point. 'What's that?'

'What is what?'

I stick my finger to the pod. 'That. The moss or mould or whatever it is crawling all over Grea's pod.'

Citlali follows my pointing, not because the avatar needs to *see* but because that's how she's been programmed, to appear as human as possible. I don't know why anyone really thought that was necessary, since a third of the crew *aren't* human and no one bothered to program Citlali to make the qwans or rucnarts more at home. I guess they figured there wasn't much point, or maybe there wasn't enough time. The *Citlali* was one of the first deep-space ships, designed before the war broke out. Jim Engineer likes to remind everyone he was there when they eventually started construction, as the war was winding down. And right about then, everyone was still struggling to think of the "kin" as more than really smart animals.

I mean, I guess that's a hazard when two of the species that almost wiped you out look like really big Old Terran birds and cats, but you'd have to be an idiot not to see the intelligence in their eyes. The war sorted that.

'Grea Darzi's stasis unit is functioning within parameters.'

'There's *fug* in my sister's unit. That's not normal.'

'My sensors do not indicate any "fug" in the pod.'

'But it's right there!' I poke the plasglas, shaking another clump of mould loose.

'My sensors do not—'

'Your sensors are fucked. There is *fug* in my sister's pod and you can't see it!' I yell the last in Citlali's face. It feels good, even if it doesn't actually mean much. Citlali doesn't care, *can't* care no matter how well she's been programmed to simulate emotion. Maybe if the spit flying from my mouth had splattered in her core instead of the deck, she might do more than blink at me. But the core isn't here. No one is here except me.

A fuzzy blue critter scoots across the deck plating, heading for the spit glistening on floor. Okay, so no one is here except me and the *critters* and if you're including them you may as well include Citlali, as useless as she is right now.

And right now, I'm not including them. The brief moment of satisfaction that came with swearing at the avatar is fading, draining out of my toes as the cold, hard grate of the decking digs into my feet. It sucks the warmth out of me, and I shiver, but that's not the worst of it. The worst of it is invading my head. Silence. So much silence. Not the kind that assaults your ears, but the kind that slithers up your spine and knocks on your skull.

The kind that tells you you're all alone.

That *I'm* all alone.

CHAPTER THREE

Screw being alone.

That was the thought that got me moving again and on the hunt for someone who could actually help. There was something wrong with the AI, that much was as obvious as gravity, and someone needed to fix her. I was about as good with fixing shit as I was at operating the stasis pods. Of course, getting out of stasis had been the easy part.

Thanks, Onah. Not.

The stasis unit is a six-metre-long rectangle that houses my family's pods. Four pods side-by-side, a curving bulkhead creating the ceiling and the opposite wall. One end is a door and the other is another bulkhead. It's got the only decoration in the otherwise bland unit with its not-quite-white walls. Big red letters are painted on it, each one the length of my forearm. "Emergency supplies", it reads.

It's not quite the last thing I saw before Mum sealed me in my pod, but it's not far off. I try not to think about why it's there, or why we might need the supplies behind it. Sometimes, just sometimes, I wish I hadn't been born in space where everything outside the *Citlali's* bulkheads would kill me.

The other end of the unit is a thick, round door. And it won't bloody open.

'Come on, Citlali, let me out!'

'The door is open Kuma.'

'It. Is. Not!' I spit each word out as I push against the steelcrete.

There's sweat trickling down my spine. I've been at this for a while now, since right after I finished screaming at the avatar. Not my proudest moment. I give the door one final shove, gripping the latch in both hands and straining with every muscle in my body. Which really isn't saying that much. Mum's always at me to spend more time with the other kids in the gym, but... Ugh. Scrawny is as scrawny does I'd say, right before I remind her that an exosuit doesn't care if my muscles bulge like Mac's or not. Then Dad'll say something about not always having an exosuit and Grea...

The tightness floods back to my chest, rushing from the silence in my head. I've never been unable to sense anybody before and it's so... empty. So still.

I bang my forehead against the door. *Not now. Freak out later, get the door open.*

Get the door open.

That light suddenly pouring out of my ears? That's the glow going off in my head.

'Shit.' Sometimes I'm an idiot. Grea will argue that I'm *always* an idiot, but she's biased. I push my mind away from thoughts of my sister. We're not thinking about her right now, we're thinking about getting out of the stasis unit so I can track down Jim Engineer and tell him his precious AI is shit-for-brains fucked.

It's right after Mae Lu finishes drilling emergency revival procedures into our heads, that Jim doubles down on the boredom with a "refresher" course on stasis units. I never really get past the bit where he drones on about how each unit is a self-sustaining lifeboat and how to... blah, blah, blah. That's the point where I tend to sneak off. But Dad caught me one day and well, he made Mae Lu seem nice. Which is why now, I remember there's an emergency door release.

I'm on my knees on the deck, twisting the little button that should... A pop of air and then a section of the door comes out in my hands. It's not an *actual* section of the door, just a plate. Behind it, nestled in a cut-out the size of my head, is a square handle. The emergency release. There's writing here too. "Twist and pull."

I grip it with both hands, set my feet and twist. The handle doesn't budge.

A thought sneaks into the back of my mind that maybe I should have listened to Mum about the gym, but I ignore it in favour of setting my feet and twisting harder. I throw everything I have into it, from my toes to my teeth. In fact, I reckon if I tighten my jaw any harder my teeth are going to shatter and then—

There's a groan and then I'm flying forward, and it's not the jaw clenching that's going to pulverise my teeth, it's the decking. My nose smacks into the floor, my chin and forehead not far behind. I'm going to have grate marks imprinted on my face for the rest of eternity, but at least the door's open, or partly open.

'Kuma, are you well?'

I really wish the AI would stop asking that. 'No,' I mutter and pick myself up. That's when I notice the blood on my lip and the droplets on the floor. I run my tongue over my teeth to check they're still there. Everything seems fine except for the numbness in my lip. Out the corner of my eye I notice critters rolling toward me, come to clean up yet more biological muck. I've never really seen them this diligent before, swarming on every little speck of dirt like they don't have anything else to do. Maybe they don't. The crew's not exactly meant to be awake yet.

Guess that makes me special.

The handle's popped out of its hollow. Once again, I wrap my hands around it, but instead of twisting this time I pull. The pull comes easier, or maybe it was as hard as the twist but I was expecting it? I don't know and I don't really care, the only thing that's important is that the stasis door is open. It rolls aside, opening up onto darkness.

When I said darkness, I hadn't mean that comforting kinda dark with the soft glow of distant light, or even the slightly more nerve-wracking darkness of a full-on blue out. The light from the stasis unit is far behind me, so far behind I can't even pick out the soft residual glow of where it might have been.

This darkness is absolute.

I might as well be walking down the corridor with my eyes shut, except there'd be more light then, even if it was only imagined.

And it would really have stuffed up following the map on my palm unit.

And that would have made finding Jim Engineer's pod kinda interesting. And not in the good way.

The *Citlali* shouldn't be this dark. There are all sorts of lights on a ship like this. Emergency lights. Lift lights. Display lights. Lights that come on when you have to go for a pee at night. Lights that simply are. Even the walls glow, a faint sheen that's only perceptible when it's not there. Hell, the *critters* glow. But there's none of that here, nothing save what's on the screen floating above my palm, and even that is barely enough to make out the deck plating.

The corridor I'm in winds around in a gentle curve with the spokes of the hallways cutting through it. The curve isn't something you'd really notice, not where I am, on the outer ring of Stasis deck, where my family's unit is, but once you wander down one of the spokes, toward the Core, the curve gets really obvious.

I follow the map down one of those spokes. Jim Engineer should be somewhere in the middle ring, not quite as protected as the inner rings – reserved for the sick folk and really important people – but doing better than the Darzis. Engineers being a little harder to come by than xenobiologists, or at least that's what Dad says.

And you know, I get it, I really do. If a meteorite hits the ship, it's the engineers you don't want getting blown into space, since they're the ones who can put the ship back together and all.

I hope I find Jim soon.

As much as the darkness bothers me, it's the cold and silence that feeds the creepy-crawlies nesting behind my ribs. There is *nothing* in the corridor, not even the hum of the *Citlali's* engines or the hush of the air cyclers. Every sound echoes, from my boots on the deck to the rustle of my clothes. Not even the AI is around. I left its avatar in the unit, waiting in the doorway like she was waving me off to war or something. And the cold... my breath frosts on the air and my nose is a leaky block of ice. I keep wiping it on my sleeve but it keeps dripping. I'd be worried the enviro systems weren't working, except I haven't suffocated yet and my toes haven't fallen off, so there's got to be something on.

'Come on, come on, come on.' I mutter to myself to keep the silence at bay, but each word booms and echoes. Somehow the echo makes the silence worse, talking back to me in my own voice, but different. Hollow. Lost. Ghostly. Reminding me of Mum and Dad and Grea in their pods. Thinking of them turns my thoughts to the rest of the crew in their pods, floating in stasis gel while they wait for *Citlali* to cross the cold dark between solar systems.

They're all around me, silent as the dead. It's freaking me out, and if the memory of the biting thing in my mind and the sharp sting of fear in Onah's wasn't making a knot at the back of my skull, I'd try reaching out to them. Skim their emotions and invade their privacy merely to reassure myself they're still alive. I swallow and make a turn at the next ring, trying to keep my eyes off the dark outlines of circular doors, each one another stasis unit. There could be corpses behind those doors. Dead people that I once knew.

A name pops up on the map and I stop. Macario. Mac.

My best friend is in there. Should I go in, try to wake him up?

The temptation is strong, but then I think of Grea and the fug, and then, instead of Grea, I imagine Mac curled up in his pod, and the pit in my chest yawns.

I scuttle back from the hatch, breathing hard. It takes me awhile to bring my breathing under control and when I do, my heart's still pounding, almost, but not quite filling the silence. I swallow it back and straighten my shoulders.

I need to find Jim Engineer.

His unit is up ahead. Another hundred metres and I'm there,

standing in front of the portal, pressing the release. Frankly, I don't know why I bothered.

Like in my unit, nothing happens. The controls are as dead as a black dwarf star.

I'm down on my knees again, pushing at the emergency panel embedded in the door, the deck icy even through my pants.

The panel pops out with a hiss of air, but only a few millimetres. I scratch at the opening, trying to hook my fingernails between the panel and the door. I manage to grab it, just a little, and pull. It doesn't budge.

I'm getting really sick of things not budging.

I try again, digging my fingernails in as deep as they'll go, setting my forehead against the steelcrete and bracing my whole body to *pull*.

And land on my butt with a hot, ragged pain in my index finger. I stick it in my mouth, tasting blood from a torn fingernail as I inspect the panel.

'Fuck.'

It hasn't budged. Not so much as a nanometre.

Sitting back and kicking the door is like spitting at *Citlali's* avatar. It makes me feel better but doesn't do a whole lot of good. And it doesn't make me feel better for long. The hollow echo of boot on hatch makes the silence deeper, playing again and again through the empty corridors. Alone, alone, alone it says.

I kick the door again to show the silence I don't care.

I'm sure it believes me as much as the pit in my chest does.

I need a pry bar to peel the panel away and get at the emergency release. Anything stronger than the keratin in my fingernails will do. I think.

I hope.

That's what I'm telling the panic building in my chest. That's what I'm telling myself. So that's what I'm going to do.

Now if only I knew where to find a pry bar.

I'm on my feet, jabbing at the raised square of flesh in the bend of my elbow that activates my palm unit. The subdermal's pretty basic and I probably should have taken the time to grab the biocomp out of my locker, but it'll do. The screen pops back up above my palm, the map with it. It's only a partial map, but it's better than nothing. The *Citlali* AI may be frizting, where it's not down altogether, but the subdermal still works a treat. Too bad most of its functions are tied to the ship. The only reason I have the map is because I downloaded it before going to stasis/sleep.

There's a maintenance locker on every deck, tools to be used in emergencies, or when you can't be stuffed trudging up to Engineering. I head for the centre of Stasis. The lockers are scattered all over the place, not always in the same location. There should be one on this ring but the spoke is around the corner and the Core not far from that, and there's always a locker there.

I should probably know the layout of the ship better; I've spent my entire life aboard *Citlali*. Like. My. Entire. Life. But everything's different in the dark, and Stasis has never been one of my favourite places. All the empty pods, all that time spent doing nothing except dreaming and sleeping. Waking up a centimetre taller than when you went to sleep. It's pretty disturbing, even for me. So I'm following the map, using it half as a guide and half for the light it casts.

The thump of my boots on the deck continues to echo, but I'm trying to ignore that. Focusing instead on the first time Dad took me planet-side.

I'd stepped out of the shuttle, watched my boots hit the moon's surface with a lazy crunch, glanced up and… freaked. It was the sky. No amount of lying on your back, gazing up at the Atrium's holographic clouds can really prepare you for *that*. Or, at least, that's what Mum tried to tell me while Grea laughed her arse off.

I've gone EVA before but staring up at that thin blue sky was different from floating in space. It felt like I was going to fall into it like… rage. What? No, that's not right. That rage isn't even *mine*.

I stop, rub my eyes and try to sort the pounding in my head.

There's a wave of emotion in there that's not mine. It's strong and has that sharp jangle only the kin have. Somewhere in my daydreaming it crept up on me like the scent of Mum's cooking, gentle and patient, but now it's a roar commanding me to listen.

Someone's awake. Someone besides *me*, is awake!

It's a rucnart, one of the gigantic feline-like tree-kin, that much is obvious from the roar, but I reach back, opening myself up to it.

Opening yourself up to a rucnart is like putting your hand in its mouth. Kinda stupid and best not attempted without medical supervision, but I'm desperate.

Of all of the kin, rucnarts are the most volatile. The qwans are crafty, their minds honed to icy daggers while the tree-kin – the rucnarts – are roiling balls of barely-leashed violence, pushing menace ahead of them like a star pushes light. Even if they weren't the height of a human and twice as long, with six legs and all the claws and teeth to match, you'd leave them alone.

But like I said, I'm desperate.

An empath doesn't listen so much as *feel*. Anger. Pain. Fear. The rucnart's emotions rocket into me one by one, each hitting harder than the last, pounding at the barrier between what is me and what is not.

My knees tremble. The fear is an ugly yellow wave winding around my heart while the anger wraps around the fear, tries to pry it free, and the pain... The sound that comes out of my throat isn't me, it's small and scared and everything the mind behind the command doesn't want to experience. I try to shove the emotions away, try to block them from my psyche, but the other mind *pushes*. I push back. It *pushes* again, harder this time, trying to escape its pain by giving it to me. But it's not my pain and I won't take it. I. Won't.

Shutting my psyche down takes more effort than it should, leaving me breathing hard in the darkness, the glow from the map scrunched up against my chest. There aren't many aboard *Citlali* strong enough to match me, not even among the kin, or so I've been told (not even I'm stupid enough to challenge a rucnart or qwan to a psionic weigh-off) but that'd been close. And I can't help but wonder who it was.

Slowly, carefully, I reach back along the remnants of the link, trying to find who it belongs to. The anger snaps at me first, sharp glistening teeth trying to sink into my brain. I make myself slippery and ghost-like and sidle past it and the teeth latch on to nothing. The emotions get thicker the closer I am to the source. Like before, they try to wrap me up and pin me in place, but like before I flit past. The pain comes next and then the fear.

Slipping into a rucnart's mind is nothing like slipping into Mum's or sharing thoughts with Onah. Mum is... well, Mum. Warm and comforting, reminding me of home. I've never really shared Onah's mind before. We've talked, like in the Dreaming, him picking thoughts out of my head and me picking thoughts out of his, but being *in* his mind? Where there's an entire world between human and Jørgen minds, there's a galaxy between Jørgen and the native Jørans we're modelled after. We feel different, for one. Human minds, even the mostly-human ones, are... static. They have colour and flavour but they don't *move* like Jørgen minds do, don't snap and hiss.

Our minds, Jørgen minds, are restless knots of energy, always moving, glowing even on the psionic plane we call the eter. And Jøran minds... well, take the restlessness of a human-Jøran hybrid and slide it all the way up to one trillion.

Even skimming the rucnart's mind is like being in a hurricane. She sweeps me up and whirls me around, the force and restlessness of her psyche trying to hook claws under my shields, trying to tear them away and... get *in*? Underneath all the pain and fear and anger, there was desperation.

The rucnart, p'Endr, was trapped inside her pod. That realisation pulls me out of her clutches, landing me back in my own body before the next thought goes through my mind. P'Endr was awake, not in some kind of induced hibernation, but awake. Eyes open with goo down her throat and in her lungs, watching as the same fug that's crawling over my sister's pod, crawls over hers. I shudder. For a nanosecond, I'd felt the fug clumping in her fur, swimming in the stasis gel, tasted it as it floated in her mouth. I can still taste it on my tongue – cold with the sharp tang of copper but something else as well, something that reminds me of maggots.

Nausea rides up my throat. I gag.

I have to get p'Endr out. That decision isn't quite mine; I can tell by the way it burrows into my brain, like a slither of ice seeking out my heart. As short as my contact was, p'Endr managed to plant a command. I could ignore it, pluck it out and trash it like one of the worms on Ag deck. But it wouldn't do any good.

P'Endr didn't need to give me a command. I'm already racing toward her.

CHAPTER FOUR

The map doesn't work, but I don't need it. The stream of pain coming from p'Endr is its own map, pulling me down the corridor like a lodestone in my gut. I sprint past a spoke, following the pain, only to skid to a halt, pinwheeling my arms as my feet keep going while the rest of me is wrenched back the way I've come.

I dive down the spoke, away from the core. Silence is no longer pressing on my ears. The TRANG TRANG TRANG of my boots on the deck are drowning it out, competing for space with the thump thump thump of my heart and p'Endr throwing herself against my shields.

She's one of the older rucnarts, with a heavy dose of white around her muzzle and frosting her red and sand-coloured coat. She's lean too, with the short, almost bobbed tail of the desert clans and the overwhelming strength to match.

The closer I get, the harder it is to shut her out. She's pounding against my psyche, clawing at my shields, trying to climb in my head. Panic is riding her hard and she's throwing it at me with everything she's got. It's making the commands she's trying to force through my shields, sticky – like psionic napalm, trying to burn through my resolve. I push her back, again and again and again, but the distance between us is no longer enough to buffer the power of her psyche and as strong as I am...

I skid around another corner, hanging onto the bulkhead to help slingshot me around and to keep me upright. Trying to keep p'Endr out is taking everything I have now, leaving nothing behind for my knees to keep me up or my feet to keep pounding the deck. I try to reach out to her, pushing all the calm and assurance that's left in my bones, giving up what's left in me to get her out of my head. A minute or a few seconds, that's all I need. All I need.

I *push* the emotions, smooth and blue and deep, trying to smother the raw, jangling fear, the panic and pain that's taken over p'Endr's mind. I sense her on the other end, the *emote* crashing over her psyche like a cooling wave, soothing the raw, bleeding skin of her mind. The fear beats back, bucking under my blanket of calm. I dig deep into my anima, my core, pulling on every last drop of power and pouring it into the *emote*.

Empaths can't form command spheres. Creating psionic packets of instruction that control another's actions is a skill that belongs to telepaths, those with the ability to hear thoughts. The tree and air-kin use it to program the critters aboard the ship, waking every ten ship years during stasis/sleep to reinforce and update them. It's a skill rare among Jørgens, and feared by most. But empaths miss out on it all together.

But what we lack, we more than make up for with other skills. Emoting is a Jørgen skill, no one really understands why us hybrids can do it and the kin can't. Everyone agrees it's got something to do with the human part of our genetics, but humans are such psionic nulls that no one can agree on what. Some of the psi researchers back on Jørn thought it had something to do with how our brains are wired, or at least that's what the records say. No one's really bothered to keep researching aboard *Citlali*. There wasn't much point until Grea and I were born. All the Jørgens that signed onto the crew were telepaths to one degree or another, and after... Well, the whole *emoting* thing? I'm not supposed to be doing it.

You see, where command spheres are scary, most telepaths can defend against them, plus the qwans would let the rucnarts eat us if we, you know, broke the "no command sphere" rule. You can't defend against *emoting* though. Not unless you have a little bit of empath in your DNA.

Even a psionic null can tell when a telepath is messing with their minds, there's this kinda *push*, a perception of something alien in your skull, something that doesn't belong. You may not perceive it right away, but you tend to notice it when the command sphere unfurls and you start doing shit you had no intention of doing. But an empath, we kinda ride in on the air cruising into your lungs and set up shop in your limbic system, whispering in your ear and tweaking your heart strings. There's nothing *alien* about a good emote, and if we do it right, you'll never even know we were there.

You pick a fight with your mum? That's all you, or rather the emotional reaction I set off in your amygdala.

And that's why I'm not supposed to do it, at least not anymore. No one really worried about it when I was a kid because my emotes were so obvious, but now... Let's just say I'm good at what I do. Not even Grea can out-emote me.

I've never tried to emote a rucnart though. It's not so much sliding in on a breath of air, but grinding over an asteroid with my tongue, all rough edges and colours that don't make sense. And while I emote, I'm dodging the claws and teeth trying to rip me apart and take over my mind. A little part of me, the only part not occupied with keeping p'Endr off my psionic back, tells me it could be worse, I could be trying keep Onah out my head. The tree-kin may be able to rip my chest open and eat my heart in ten seconds flat, but the air-kin are the true psionic powerhouses aboard *Citlali*. Dad says that only the swatai, the water-kin, are stronger, which is why there aren't any on board. That, and we don't have enough water for them. He seemed really glad about that.

P'Endr has all the adrenalin that fear and panic can lend her. Not much can keep me out of someone's mind, but that will do it well enough. Heightened emotion is tough to overcome, kinda like trying to colour over black with yellow. Add in adrenalin and you have a mind so focussed on one thing that it's tough to convince it to let go. Still, I'm getting somewhere. There's enough room in my brain to consider things other than keeping p'Endr out now, enough for me to spare some thought for my body.

I push away from the bulkhead and stumble down the corridor. The spaces between hatches is getting wider, meaning I must be in the Jøran section, where the units have to be bigger to accommodate their size. I can almost see p'Endr now. The trail of her fear shimmers in my mind's eye, leading me straight to the round hatch, which is good and bad.

Good because I've found her. Bad because her emotions are punching me in the face, and the emote I laid over her? She smashes it.

The backlash has me on my arse before I'm really sure what's happened, and then I can't really *think* about what's happened because—

Old Terra. My heart's racing a million parsecs an hour, pounding its way out of my chest and all I can see, all I can feel is the grey-green fug wriggling down my throat and eating my fur. I lash out at the hatch, claws leaving long furrows in the clear, human-made glass, trying to catch the red square in front of my muzzle, but they slide through. I yowl and thrash, choking on the blue liquid even as blood stains it red. The need for oxygen is burning my lungs, the fug eating my insides and—

I'm released. A rush of liquid, a gasp of air. For a second, the sensation of the cold on my fur merges with the deck beneath my arse, and it's hard to separate the sensations, hard to peel p'Endr from my mind. She's out of the pod, panic and fear still ruling her emotions, giving them strength and making them sticky, but the relief, the air in her nose and the hard steelcrete under her paws, gives me a second to myself. A second is all I need to slam my shields in place.

I flop back on the deck. I'm me again. The pounding of my heart is my own, so too the sweat on my brow. All me. P'Endr is out of her pod, behind the door, still gasping for breath as the stasis gel exits her lungs. That much is clear, but she's no longer trying to swallow me whole.

I frown. Is she *too* quiet? Rucnarts aren't exactly peaceful, especially when you do something stupid like sprinkle their dens with pepper, and coming out of stasis with fug eating your fur and blood—

Blood. The word pops into my mind on the memory of the stasis gel stained red, the coppery taste of it on p'Endr's tongue. Oh shit.

All the adrenalin that fuelled p'Endr is now mine, pushing my heart faster, getting me on my feet, my hands pushing at the emergency release, grabbing the handle. Every muscle in me strains, my lungs scream for air and my vision goes white, but the hatch pops open.

It takes years for the hatch to roll aside enough for me to squeeze through. I don't hesitate, not even when I'm halfway through and a memory of Dad telling me never to approach an injured Jøran blooms in my brain. Claws and fangs and rage, that's what he said, all of it searching for a squishy human – hybrid or no – to sink into.

Stupidity overrides fear though, that and the need to get inside the unit. Is it p'Endr's need or mine? Does it matter? I'm in the unit now. The lighting's on the fritz, only the dim, yellow-orange emergency lights illuminate the pods, the flood of blue-green gel and the rucnart sprawled over the decking. She's on her side, like she's too tired, and maybe she is. She doesn't lift her head when I finish squeezing through, doesn't flick an ear. I can hear her breathing though, long wheezy inhale and shuddering exhales. Her emotions are quiet, too quiet, like all that fear and adrenalin have done what I couldn't, and zoned her out, except...

It doesn't feel right. I step further into the unit. Now that I can see her – paws as big as my face, the gleam of fangs – Dad's voice is making my steps slower, raising the caution that my concern obliterated. Gingerly, half an eye on the hallway beyond the hatch, I step around p'Endr, until I can see her eyes. They're open, all four of them, but half-lidded and her upper eyes, the ones kin only open when they're playing with your mind, are unfocused, the slit pupils large, the usually red iris clouded. She sees me and her lower eyes, the regular everyday ones, open a little wider. She twitches, forelegs and sides heaving as if she wants to sit up. For a second she's almost there, forelegs folding and head rising off the ground, but then it's like she gets stuck, frozen, and she crashes back to the deck.

She wheezes again. The sound is different this time, heavier, like she has to work harder to move her lungs in and out.

'It's okay,' I say. 'It's the stasis gel. It'll dissolve in a moment.'

P'Endr gives me a look, and I lower my shields enough to let her in.

Pain. The taste of blood. A rattle in her chest; breathing like the fabric of her lungs is full of holes. A sense of something *wrong*, so very wrong.

I stumble back, shutting her out of my brain with a sharp SNAP of my shields. My face is cold, like the blood has rushed out of it, and I'm suddenly light-headed. That's when I notice the red stain around her muzzle, the pink froth caught in the crease of her jaws.

'Citlali!' I yell the AI's name. It echoes off the walls loud enough to make p'Endr flatten her ears.

Nothing. No pop of light, no shimmer of her avatar materialising beside me.

I spin around in case she's behind me.

'Citlali!' I yell again. 'Citlali!'

Nothing, nothing save p'Endr lungs rattling behind me, the deep, chest-tearing cough, the whine. I spin back around.

She's hacking up blood and... other things. Whatever it is, it's thick and grey, chunky almost. That's not right. I know it in my bones, know it the way p'Endr knows it, and the knowledge makes me cold.

'What do I do?'

She stares at me and there's panic there, but it's dim and tired. I sense her, beyond my shields, and that same tiredness is in her thoughts, soaking them, making them slow. She's trying to tell me something, and so I open myself up again, not quite all the way, but enough for her to enter my psyche like Onah did, but where the fug was a sickness hidden behind the white/black of his mind, p'Endr's green/lilac was being eaten away, her animas full of holes. The fug couches everywhere in her psyche, coating the bright colour with its ugly film.

A thought packet sits on the edge of her thinking, as clouded as the rest of her mind. She holds it out to me. Slowly, with all the caution of Dad's warnings sounding in my head, I reach for it.

It tastes like mould, coating the back of my tongue with an ugly, cloying film, dulling my senses. I try to clear it out, to scrape the mould out of my psyche. It's like scraping crud out of the cyclers, the thick goopy stuff sticking to my hands, but once it's off the message underneath is clear and bright. The thought packet dissolves in my brain, the knowledge within sinking into my psyche like it had always been there.

It's a memory.

I'm floating in the eter, the minds of the crew bright stars amongst the darkness of space. The humans shift slowly, the Jørgens are restless nodes of energy zipping and sliding between them, always moving, disturbing the psionic plane with their restlessness. And there, points of being hidden behind a wall only other Jørans can see, are the kin. Tree and Air merged in the Aer, a world constructed from memories and the power of their combined psyches, where they can leap through the great trees of mountain forests and fly through the clear desert skies.

The Aer changes, a shudder disturbing the earth, a note of *wrongness* singing through the leaves.

It tastes like rot, and as p'Endr stands atop a stony outcropping and lifts her nose to the breeze, she sees it. A grey-green stain rushing over the forest, swallowing tree and air-kin alike. The memory shudders and for a moment, barely long enough to take note, I'm in a blank spot, like part of the memory has been cut away, everything except an ancient sense of *knowing* and fear.

Then the blank spot resolves and I'm back as p'Endr, but she's no longer atop the outcropping. Time has shifted and she's perched in the lower branches of a forest behemoth, fighting the fug. She growls and snaps at the writhing grey-green carpet, leaping off the branch to confront the intruder on the ground, but it pays her no mind, just keeps rolling on. She sees h'Spa swallowed by the fug. Hears him howl, senses his pain and confusion before she senses nothing from him at all.

Overhead, a shadow breaks from the trees, wings beating furiously as the air-kin, as Onah, breaks for the edge of the Aer. The fug almost seems to *look* and then stretches toward the fleeing shape.

P'Endr strikes, ignoring the pain as she sinks her jaws into the fug. The enemy screams, the sound piercing her ears. She snarls and shakes her head, not letting go until the enemy is focussed on her, then she runs. The fug chases, nipping at her heels until it corners her on the rocky outcropping overlooking the forest. The forest is no longer green. It's dull and grey, the edges fading, the trees becoming indistinct as the fug swallows it until only the iridescent sphere, the last stronghold of the kin, in its centre, remains. It's already stained, the fug climbing up its sides like an ugly mould. If it doesn't hold—

Fear, a hot, all-consuming wave holds her still. And that's when she's caught.

The stain snags her tail, she feels it bite and tries to spin, to confront it with her teeth, but she's stuck. The fug is sliding over her paws, sticking her to the ground.

The memory ends.

I blink, my vision dark as my brain readjusts to using my eyes.

That...

There are no words, only the lingering sense of p'Endr's memory, the fading kin and the fug writhing over the forest. The fear is the worst of it. It's not the same pounding, adrenalin-fuelled explosion as before. It doesn't hammer at my psyche trying to get in. It doesn't need to. It's already sitting in my chest. Cold and hard, but tiny, like it's hiding from itself. Right over my heart.

I rub my chest, crouch beside p'Endr and—

She's dead.

Unmoving. Eyes open, mouth gaping, tongue slack and hanging between her jaws.

Dead.

I don't...

I don't know.

I just...

CHAPTER FIVE

The pry bar shatters. Like, explodes into a million tiny pieces. Right in my face. Up my nose, down my shipsuit. Everywhere. I swear I'm going to be spitting out plasform for the next week. The front of my shipsuit is covered with the stuff and it's going to take forever to get it out of the little creases in my hands. But that's nothing to the carnage around me. The deck is littered with the remnants of other pry bars.

My hands hurt and there are little nicks and cuts all over my palms, little streaks of blood on my shipsuit where I've wiped them. The streaks are already fading into the fabric, the molecules broken down and stored away by the nanites. My stomach is threatening to eat through my spine

So now I'm sitting on my butt, staring at the shards in my hand, hoping they're going to develop nanites and reassemble themselves. I stare really hard. Hold my breath even. But no. The shattered bits of white plasform remain shattered.

Damn it. Old Terra, damn it. And then maybe Jørn too and Onah and Mum and—

Take a breath, Kuma, you're not going to be able to curse the pry bar back together. I close my eyes. In through the nose, out through the mouth. Except that reminds me of Citlali, scrunching her nose up as she pretended to breathe.

'Crap.' I'm back staring at the remains of the bar. I'd finally found the maintenance locker, jimmied it open (because of course, it wasn't working either) and dug through a web of... I don't know what it was. Funky grey-green stuff that reminded me of the fug wriggling over my sister's pod and p'Endr's—

No. I wasn't thinking of that.

The fug clung to *everything* and I had to pull it off the pry bar. It stuck to me as well, clinging to my fingers and seeming to slide over my hands. Even now, the memory of it makes me want to gag. There was something wrong about the web, something that bit at the edges of my psyche.

But I'm not worrying about that now. No. Now I'm worrying about the pry bar and the emergency panel between me and Jim's pod. There's a dent in the top, a tiny lip peeled away from the door. When I press my face to the door and peer down, I can see the emergency release handle, but no way am I getting my hand down there.

I plonk back on the decking. The bar shouldn't have shattered like that. I don't know much about engineering but I know that much. I take another look at the pieces in my hands. Maybe that funky web weakened it. What am I going to do now? I don't know how long I've been at this, but I've hit every locker on Stasis from the inner ring to the outer. Some of them didn't even have doors anymore, only the grey-green web. The tools in those ones had been so much dust. Others had appeared okay, but the bars crumbled as soon as I picked them up. Only those from the last few on the outer ring lasted long enough for me to wedge them against the door.

What *was* that web?

There are no critters on the ship that make them, at least none I know about and I spend a *lot* of time down in the Hatchery, much to my sister's disgust. She really hates it when I send the fuzzy ones after her.

In fact, there'd been tiny skeletons small enough to be critters tangled up amongst the yellow strands. Like the pry bars, they'd disintegrated.

If I can't get to Jim Engineer, then I need to get to the Core. The

Citlali isn't just one AI, it's made up a bunch of smaller AIs, each one overseeing a specific task, but they're all controlled by Core.

That avatar in the stasis unit? That was a fragment of Core, or rather, a fragment of the fragment that looked after all the units on Stasis.

Here's the thing with the *Citlali*. It's got a personality disorder, in that it's eight AIs in one. The ship is too big for one computer to control on its own, at least without it being *really* big, so all the ship's functions got split up and shared around.

Core runs the ship. She's like the brains of the brains, making sure everything is running like it should, and telling off the other bits of herself – the sub-AIs – when they fuck up. Which isn't often, and it's not like she grounds them or anything, or like they fuck up that much. Just sometimes. And really, the fuck ups aren't all that big, not like when I accidentally put my shoes in the food cyclers and everyone had to eat protein mush for a week. Nope, the kind of things the sub-AIs get wrong are like being a nanosecond behind with their reports. Core is all over that, which I guess is why things never get as bad as shoes in the food cyclers.

Long story short, if you want to get something done, Core's where it's at. So that's where I'm going.

I hope the fug hasn't eaten the door.

The fug has eaten the door.

Not all of it, but enough to make getting in kinda tricky.

The big round hatch looks like it's had a buzz cut, which is, you know, unusual for steelcrete. There's not a hint of the off-white bulkhead under the grey-green carpet. It's the same all the way around. I walked the thirty-metre circuit that makes up the inner ring of Stasis to make sure, picking my way over the trails of fug stretching across the deck.

There were holes in some places, metre-thick sections of the bulkhead eaten away like it was cheese. Some of the holes were big enough to squirm through and I might have tried, if not the faint glimmer of an energy field.

The blue glow extends around the big hatch that leads to Core. It ripples and pops, and it doesn't take a genius to figure out that the AI has put some kind of electronic shield around it. Okay, so maybe it *does* take a genius. I rub my hand. My entire arm is still numb from the jolt that just about shocked me out of my skin. But hey, it's not like I was *expecting* a forcefield or anything. I didn't even know the *Citlali* could do that. Not outside of the labs at least.

The fug's writhing all over the bulkhead around the Core. It doesn't appear like it's moving and then you realise that it's taken over the control panel and, Old Terra, you better get out of the way 'cause it's coming for you too.

There are tiny holes in the steelcrete of the bulkhead, almost too hard to see, except for the pops of energy coming off the shield.

I'm standing as close to the centre of the ship as I can get, right in the middle of Stasis. The inner ring, where all the really important people are, isn't all that big, I can walk around it in two minutes. Command's stasis unit is behind me, and the XOs. There's a bright blue hatch on the other side that holds all the crew who hadn't made it out of sickbay before stasis/sleep, and the Chief Medic (who's not Mae Lu, 'cause then she wouldn't have enough time to nag us juniors). Core is right in the middle of it all, a circular room three decks high and thirty metres across, holding court with Command and all the sick people.

The inner ring is meant to be the safest place aboard the *Citlali*; buried in the centre of the ship, more protected even than the middle rings, where Jim Engineer is. It's why the Core's here and the command staff right next to it, so when shit goes wrong they can get down to the business of saving people.

That hasn't turned out so well.

I don't turn to face Command's unit. Lyn Captain is kinda cool and her kids aren't that bad for stinky little toddlers.

There's no forcefield on the stasis units, no fuzz and pop of electricity to keep the fug at bay. I can wriggle through the hole in their hatch and I would have, except I don't want to hurl again.

There was nothing in my stomach the first time and my abdomen hurts from chucking up bile and then nothing else.

Just imagining the… mess in their stasis unit is enough to roil my stomach. The memory of the shattered pods, the gel thick and frozen like some kind of decayed ooze, the arm sticking out of it, fingers clawed, is a hot, putrid-smelling coal in my mind.

I didn't even get in far enough to see the face attached to the hand. It'd taken me whole heartbeats to figure out it *was* a hand, and that'd been enough.

I was going to dream about that.

As I'd walked around the Core, I'd made a deal with myself not to look in the units with the gaping holes. Almost all of them had holes.

There are ten units on the inner ring, ten families who are meant to keep *Citlali*, keep *me* safe. I didn't peer in the units, didn't count the holes. If I don't, I don't have to know if they're dead, don't have to know if they're hanging out of their pods like the captain, clawing their way through stasis gel turned hard. If they're not dead, there's still hope, still a chance that I can *fix* this… Whatever this is.

Some part of me, the bit I'm trying to ignore, kept its own tally. Peered into every hole, saw the shadows, smelled the sweet, putrid scent of decay.

It's not easy ignoring your own thoughts, but I'm doing my best. I'm pretending it's Grea knocking on my brain, getting back at me for covering her bed in critters, or sneaking into her not-as-secret-as-she-thought stash of chocolate and replacing it with cheese.

She hates cheese.

I've stood still too long, trying to ignore the creeping sensation on the back of my neck, not watching the fug.

I can't save Grea from here. I can't get into the Core. I can't wake the captain or the XO or… or… The hesitation is an invitation for my brain to show me all the things I didn't want to see.

No. No. No.

I have to get out of here.

There's nothing I can do for them, nothing for me here but ghosts and the smell of death.

I stumble back, or try. One foot moves but the other refuses.

I glance down.

Fug has slithered over my boot, greedily reaching around the sole and covering the toes, sticking it in place.

Fear blooms in my chest and gives me a surge of strength. There's a thick, meaty *THHHRIP* and I'm free.

Free and running all the way home.

There is no home, only darkness and the endless echo of my boots.

I don't know how far I ran, or even really where, just that I'm on the Outer ring, as far from the Core as I can get.

It's cold. I imagine my breath frosting on the air, the white puff trailing from my nose. It's the kind of cold that makes Mum yell at Jim Engineer for forgetting to overhaul the enviros. And then Jim checks out the controls in the quarters I share with my family, and he gets this funny expression on his face, fiddles with things a bit and tells Mum he's sorry and it's all fixed now.

No one tells Mum that Grea was "improving" the cabin's AI again and fucked up the sub systems.

Sometimes it's like my twin gets all the love.

But if she were here, if it was me stuck in the pod instead of her, she'd be doing something. Something clever, something genius. She'd be kicking the fug's spore-ridden butt, not sitting here in the dark, imagining her breath misting on the air.

I wipe my cheeks.

I've gotta get to the Core.

The fug's not going to stop me.

CHAPTER SIX

It's cold in the freight lines, colder than Stasis. My fingernails are going blue and I'm pretty sure my lips are going to fall off any second now.

To make it worse, there's a breeze. The breeze is how I know there's a cargo palette coming up behind me. There's not an actual *wind* aboard *Citlali*, those sorts of enviros are limited to Agriculture, and sometimes the Rec deck. This breeze is caused by the palettes moving through the system, pushing air in front of them like a giant cleaning bot gathering up dust. It gets stronger as the palette nears, nipping at my heels, making my hair snarl and tangle. I jump off the line.

There's no sound at first, nothing but that rush of air, but as it grows stronger, the rush becomes a hum and then a boom as the palette rips past, fast enough to catch me in its backdraft.

There are all kinds of ways to get around the *Citlali*. Most of the adults settle for the corridors and lifts, some even have mini-hovers, the qwans like to ride the rucnarts, the critters use the tubes and the kids... We've got the speedway.

Some of the older folks, the ones who actually grew up on Jørn, like to tell us about the street races, illegal gigs where people teamed up and rode their companions around the city. Everyone would be out to get everyone else, using drones and bombs to take out the competition. It always sounded kinda fun, but I reckon it's got nothing on the speedway. Not even the fastest companion can run as fast as a cargo palette with its safeties turned off. They can't go vertical either, or do a loop 'de loop. Not that there are a lot of loops on the *Citlali*, but we make do. You also can't shoot a companion out into space. Well, you can, I guess, but expecting them to come back alive would be tricky.

The speedway is how the ship moves cargo around. It's not *actually* a speedway (it's not even called a speedway), and it's not really meant to be used by humans, which I reckon was a major oversight. Command tried to keep us out of it for ages, but there's only so much they can do, and the Citlali... well, the AI didn't seem to mind us playing around in her insides. Eventually Command gave up trying to keep us out, especially when a few of the older crew got in on the action. Kinda hard to make something illegal if your second-in-command is egging your Chief Medic on.

I guess someone might have tried to get a barrier racing team going, but there aren't any striders aboard the ship. Companions big enough to ride are too big for a ship like this. Plus, the rucnarts hate them. Like, *really* hate them. Guess it's got something to do with that thing during the war. No one's ever been stupid enough to ask though. When rucnarts bite your head off, they use their teeth.

I mightn't have been able to get into Core through the front door, but there's always a back way. That's one of the things you discover on a ship like this. As simple and secure as the engineers like to make things out to be, there's always a work-around. And right now, I'm going for the indirect route.

That means hitching a ride on the speedway to the maintenance tunnels that run throughout the ship's skeleton.

The speedway is a web of square tubes with rounded corners. Three of me can lie end to end across one and *still* not touch the other side. They're as dark as Stasis except for the mag-lines – thick lines of bio-gel and steelcrete running down the middle of the bulkheads, deck and ceiling. They're glowing enough to make out the shadow-lines, where the plating fits together. I shut my palm unit off.

My map's useless now anyway. Good thing I know my way around. Mostly.

I've never actually been this way before, at least when I'm not going one twenty klicks an hour, and definitely not to get to Core. For one, it doesn't *really* go to Core, not directly; and two, Core's kinda boring. Nothing to see there but bio-gel and databanks.

The maintenance hatch I want is up ahead, I can see the star, *Citlali's* symbol, on the wall. There's something funky about it though. Instead of six sharp points, like spears thrusting from a circular centre, the star is fuzzy, like there's a layer of fog between me and the hatch… or the fug that gunked up my sister's pod. Some of the nerves I left behind in Stasis start dancing in my stomach.

I tell myself it's simply the dark and distance messing with my vision. My stomach doesn't quite believe me, but I ignore it. I wish I'd convinced Mum to let me get an optical upgrade, I could have zoomed in on the hatch, figured out if the fuzziness really was a figment of my imagination.

Not that it would matter much, I can't open a hatch by eyeballing it.

Another breeze pushes me along the tube, gentle but getting stronger with every passing second, almost like it's trying to hurry me along. And maybe it is. The hatch is on the bend, and there's not a lot of room between the mag-lines and the wall for me to avoid getting squished by a palette. I'm not worried about it though. The palettes are programmed to stop long before they hit anything, namely me.

Still, I pick up the pace as the breeze becomes a wind. The nerves are doing their jig, breaking out of my gut to climb up my spine, and whatever's coming up behind me isn't helping. It must be big, or maybe the AI is using all the lines, because now the wind is *pushing* me along, and the lines are humming, loud enough to blot out the echo of my feet. Citlali gets kinda pissed when we hold up the big loads, not that the AI is capable of true emotion, but she does a good job of faking it.

I'm running now, and not because of Citlali. The mag-lines aren't merely humming, they're glowing, all four of them getting brighter and brighter. The hatch is ahead and I can make out the fuzziness now, a grey-green mould hugging the star and edges where it meets the bulkhead.

The thought of touching it sends the nerves up my throat, along with a little bit of sick, but that hum... I don't know what it is, but the hum, the way the mag-lines are trying to burn themselves onto my eyeballs, it's scaring the shit out of me. I don't care what the safety protocols are, I'm getting out of this tube before the palettes have a chance to smear me across the bulkhead.

The wind is blowing my hair past my face, pressing the seams of my shipsuit into my back hard enough I reckon it's going to leave marks. I race the last hundred metres. My breath is coming hard and the light's so bright it's hurting my eyes. The control panel is buried under a carpet of fug. I wipe it away with both hands, resisting the urge to hurl.

The sound of the palette coming down the tube helps with that, no longer a hum but a roar. It shouldn't be doing that, and I guess that's why my hands are shaking and I'm managing to ignore the fact that the fug is now *crawling* over my hands. The damn stuff is alive, I can almost *see* it slithering up my brain stem.

'Crap, crap, crap.' I try to shake it off but the damn stuff is stickier than nano-glue. I hesitate, imagining fug eating the pry bars, the blood on p'Endr's snout, before wiping my hands on my shipsuit, leaving streaks of grey-green behind. I'm pretty sure they start moving, but I'm not paying attention. Not. Paying. Attention.

There's no time to freak out about the fug eating my clothes. The wind is strong enough to blow me over now, and I have to hang on to the edges of the hatch to stand up.

The control panel is messed up, parts of it hanging out of its casing, the holoscreen spitting little bits of light as I press my hand to it. I even see bio-gel dribbling out the bottom. It seems like it's working though and—

A siren blares. With all the force of the wind behind it, the sound knocks me off my feet, makes my vision wobbly.

That's probably what saves my life. I fall into the gap between the lines and the palette rushes past me, over me, around me. It's huge. Taking up all four mag-lines. For three heartbeats it surrounds me, a rush of sound and colour, before I'm tumbled in its backdraft.

I spend a few seconds on my back, not sure what I'm seeing, but the mag-lines are going back to their usual soft glow and the hurricane of the palette's passing has faded to nothing. I'm just glad I'm alive. And then I see the fug. Not only on the hatch but inching up the bulkhead and across the ceiling, stretching out toward the mag-line there and hugging it. It runs along either side like a weird vine, changing as it does so, growing broad, flat appendages like leaves, if leaves could slice up plasform like it were butter.

That shit is freaking me out.

'What the Old Terra is it?'

My voice echoes in the tube and no one answers, not even the Citlali, who should be around here somewhere.

That's why I'm here though, not lying around admiring the fug as I wait for another palette to flatten me.

I'm on my feet and opening the hatch. It doesn't slide aside like it should. It's a little stickier than it should be too, like something has eaten the sliders, and takes more effort to shove aside. Behind it, the tiny walkway is choked with the same webs I found in the maintenance lockers, except its thicker here and...

Okay, now I really want to back up and get outta here. The webs are *moving* and not in some breeze, because there isn't anything to push air around in the maintenance tubes. Nothing. But no one's told the fug that.

It's strung across the thin crawl space in thread-fine filaments, stretching from ceiling to deck to bulkhead. Some threads are thicker than others, more grow as I watch. But that's not what's really flipping me out. There are tendrils curling from the bulkheads like they're trying to catch something. I swallow my nerves. I really don't want to go any further. Creepy-crawly curly shit is not my thing, especially when it looks like it wants to eat me.

Unbidden comes the memory of Grea curled in a ball in her pod, of p'Endr lying on the deck of her stasis unit, eyes staring at nothing. It overlays the one of Grea, and for a moment it's not the rucnart on the deck, it's my sister.

My heart lurches. My insides turn to ice. For several long heartbeats the image stays with me, burning itself into my brain. I know before I take my next breath, the image is one I'll remember for the rest of my life. It scares me. Scares me right down to my bones. Scares me more than fug.

I'm going to hold this over Grea's head for eternity. The day I walked through creepy fug to save her from... well, fug. She's totally going to owe me.

Taking a deep breath, I plunge into the creepiness.

I should have brought a flamethrower or an envirosuit, or maybe gloves.

I gave up trying to wipe fug off my face around the same time my hand started sticking to it. Consequently, it was also about the time the fug got too thick to walk through.

Now I'm burrowing a tunnel through it, using my hands to dig through the web like it was dirt. The filaments stuck to everything. I swear there's some down my shipsuit, sliding in the gap between my ankle and my shoes. There's probably a few strands in my brain by now too. I bet they're slithering through my ears, seeking grey matter like Mac on a cheese hunt. That dude can find cheese anywhere, even the Ag stores where I hid the gouda. It was a prank. Kind of. More like a pre-prank prank. Mac's into everything and sometimes it's hard to get anything done, 'cause he's like, you know, *there* all the time. The gouda hunt kept him busy for almost an entire ship cycle. I still don't know how he tracked it down. I hid that cheese *good*. But Mac's weird.

If he were here, digging through the same fug/web he was trying to save his sister from (not that he has one), he'd probably be smiling.

I'm not. Smiling means I'll get more fug in my mouth. There's already enough of it there to coat my teeth. I've even given up trying to spit it out. Now, I'm concentrating on anything but the squirmy, wriggly sensation of it on my tongue, *anything* but the feel of it trying to slide down my throat.

Right now, 'anything' is the knot of web gripped between my hands. It's tougher than the rest of it, thicker. I grit my teeth (still safely tucked behind my lips) and yank. It doesn't budge. I give it another tug, which is about as successful as the first one and sit back on my heels.

Through the criss-crossing webs, I can make out a junction and the soft glow of a holo that *should* be the Core's hatch. Except I can't see the actual panel, only an orange halo of light where it should be. Merely a few strides between me and it. It doesn't sound like much, but the fug's a wall. I shove my hands in it and try again, straining with everything I have. Teeth, shoulders, arms, legs. *Everything.*

Pain rips through my hands; that sharp, wet, ripping kind that comes with blood.

The web stills. The tendrils freezing, the filaments no longer drifting in their imagined breeze.

This can't be good.

It isn't.

The fug turns on me like a rucnart on the hunt. Or at least, how I *imagine* they hunt. I've never actually seen it, because then I'd be dead.

Dead. Dead. Dead.

Almost like now.

I'm scrambling backwards on butt and bloody hands and the fug... It's reaching for me. Those tendrils are stretching toward my toes, tangling in my hair, rolling in the smears of red left on the deck.

'Shit. Shit. Shit.'

Going backwards isn't going very fast and the fug is *growing*, growing with a purpose. I can sense it, like an oil slick over my psyche. It's cold, mechanical, determined. I've never sensed anything like it. Whatever this shit is, it has *emotions* and that scares the crap out of me. Fug, mould, webs in my world don't *have* emotion.

A memory sneaks up on me. Not mine, one of p'Endr's. Of the fug biting her heels, the metallic alienness of it invading her bones, and a fear that seemed to reach all the way back, to pull something ancient from the depths of her mind. A memory that traced back hundreds of years and filled her with a fear sharper than the promise of death.

I shove the memory aside before p'Endr's fear becomes mine, then I squirm around in the tight space and high tail it out of that tube.

I'm back, and this time I'm armed and ready.

The speedway's quiet, no breeze, the mag-lines shedding their usual soft glow.

I heft the rifle and stare at the mess of web and tendrils that've taken over the tube while I constructed my weapon.

It isn't a flamethrower, but it'll do.

It took a while, a while in which I wondered if Grea was alright, wondered what she would do if she were here and it was me stuck in the pod, curled up against the fug. There might've also been a few moments there were I had to stuff the sobs back down my throat and wipe the tears from face when memories of p'Endr got mixed up with Grea.

In the end, after raiding every maintenance locker on Stasis, picking up anything that looked remotely useful, I figured out how to concoct a fug-killing machine. It isn't pretty and Dad'd have my head if he could see the bio-gel tendrils sticking out the side of the old multi-tool. It looks like I murdered a stunner, chopped it up and stitched it back together with a few extra parts thrown in for good measure. A holo-emitter over the muzzle, a power-pak sticking out of the rifle butt and a heap of bio-gel smeared in between. A Franken-thrower.

The Franken-thrower isn't as heavy as it appears, but it's almost a metre long and all the weight's at the muzzle end. It's going to be a bitch in the maintenance tube, especially if I have to crawl. Not that I'm planning on crawling, not with this baby.

Nope. I'm planning on burning.

I heft the Franken up against my shoulder and take a few deep breaths, trying to calm my heart and stir up the courage to kick in the star-emblazoned hatch.

In the time since I scrambled out of there like my butt was on fire (or, you know, being chased by freaky, blood-happy mould), the fug has grown, sneaking around the hatch and writhing over the freight tube like a grey-green blanket of freakiness. The hatch is kinda worn now too, the edges eaten away, pocked and ragged like they've rusted out.

So you know, steelcrete doesn't rust. In fact, last research-cycle, when Mac told me the asteroid we'd hauled into the cargo bay was rusted, I had to look up what he meant.

I know. I know. Not the time for trips down memory lane, but the thought of what's behind that bulkhead, of all those tendrils waving about and rolling in smears of my blood... Oh man, it's wigging me out. Panic is a chain around my chest, making it hard to breathe, to swallow even. I really don't want to go back in there, but I want to be alone in the middle of space even less, so I'm holding the memory of Grea close. Using the fear of her lying on the deck in a pool of stasis gel and blood, a reminder that there are worse things than fug.

I have the Franken-thrower. I can do this.

I take a deep breath, forcing my lungs to expand against the panic. I can do this.

I can.

I kick the hatch in.

The steelcrete doesn't so much crack as crumble, the door giving way like Old Terran cardboard, collapsing around my foot.

I try to pull it out.

It's stuck.

Oh shit.

I set the butt of Franken against the bulkhead and push. My foot moves an inch.

Fug is writhing all over the crumpled hatch, a foot-seeking wave of fuzzy grey-green.

Oh shit. Oh shit.

I'm hopping now, tugging and hopping. The fug is a shackle around my ankle. Another hop/tug. The crumble shifts. The fug reaches for my shipsuit. My boot pops free.

Mum only raised one time-waster (me) but I ain't wasting any time now. The Franken-thrower is at my shoulder, my finger on the trigger the heartbeat after I have both feet on the floor.

I fire.

For a second it's like nothing's happening, like I'm standing there, shooting imaginary lasers from my fingers. Which would be cool if it didn't suck so much. I keep pressing the trigger trying not to imagine all the ways I could have fucked this up.

Did I get the holo connection right? The hard-light generator? I know it's not the power-pak 'cause I remember sliding it in, hearing the little click—

Oh shit. Did I?

I'm all set to check it out when heat blasts out of the barrel. The Franken kicks against my shoulder, forcing me back a step and then the hatch is sporting a head-sized red spot. And, Old Terra, but it's *hot*. Sweat's beading on my forehead and I really wish I'd grabbed an enviro-mask as well.

But that's not what's important right now. The red spot on the door is getting bigger, the centre changing from red, to yellow and then white. The fug is shrinking away from it, the grey-green carpet flowing back through the crumbled steelcrete.

'Oh, no way Fug.' I swing the Franken toward the retreating

mould. 'Eat heat.'

Tip one, fug isn't flammable. It goes black, kinda smokes and turns to ash completely missing the bursting into flame part altogether.

Tip two, wear ear protection, 'cause it makes this high-pitched whine that drills into your ears, making them pop before it goes for your brain. My fingers spasm on the rifle, all of my muscles locking up, from the little ones around my eyes to my toes. Pain like I've never felt is lancing through my nerves, like lightning or acid or... or... It hurts too much to think.

The Franken hits the deck and I follow it. I can't help it, my body isn't mine anymore, it belongs to the pain, to the *sound*. I want to crawl into an airlock and shoot myself into space. Not because I want to die, but because then I could escape the whine, and the electric lance turning my grey-matter to mush.

Tip three. Fug is vengeful.

Darkness is swallowing my vision, and I'm reaching for it, hungry for the blessed relief of unconsciousness when a massive chunk of mould detaches from the ceiling and splots on my face.

CHAPTER SEVEN

When I wake up, I'm not in the freight tunnel, the whine is no longer squashing my brain, and there's a critter in my face.

It takes me a minute to realise critters haven't learned to levitate while I was in stasis/sleep. It's the small, thumb-sized paw between my eyes that does it. If it were levitating, it wouldn't need to balance itself with one paw while eating with the other. I'm on my back staring at a pale-yellow ceiling, rippled like it's made of a dozen head-sized tubes. A shadow moves through one of the ripples, a small round shape the size of my clenched hand.

I know that ceiling; have stared at it for hours, getting away from my sister, my dad, the crew. It's five decks below Stasis, on Ag Three.

How'd I get to one of the Agriculture decks?

The last thing I remember was passing out as a hank of fug found a new home on my face. At least I'm not dead. The how doesn't really matter.

Once that sorts itself out, other things start to filter in, like the fact the surface under me is hard and I'm lying on my back somewhere that isn't the freight tubes. The critter's blocking my view of the ceiling, so it's hard to guess where I am, but right now, I'm savouring the peace that comes from critters.

The one on my forehead is twice the size of the critters in the Stasis unit, the colour of wheat without the wild puff of fur. It *fuzzes;* not a sound or a vibration, but an awareness that melts through skin and bone to sink into the part of me that isn't human, the part that doesn't talk or think, but *feels*. The empathic part. I like critters. There's not much to them, but they're always bright and soft and happy, unlike the other lifeforms on *Citlali*. Sometimes, when Grea won't shut up or Dad is hammering me to get off my butt, I'll sneak into the Hatchery and hang out with the little dudes.

They're simple and easy to understand, and they don't nag me to make something of myself.

Warmth and fullness spread through my brain from the critter in a wave of gold that soothes the rough patches left by the fug's whine. I sigh and close my eyes again, basking in the sensation, letting it wash away the memory of lightning frying my insides.

I love critters. Love. Critters.

There's a strange feeling building in my stomach, a sickly, too-full sensation and the beginnings of nausea, like I ate Grea's not-so-secret stash of chocolate. It builds in my belly but instead of writhing up my throat and out my mouth, it spreads up and down my spine, invading my fingers and toes, making my lips numb and the skin on my back tight.

It takes me a second to realise the feeling isn't mine.

I sit up, catching the critter before it hits the deck. Others I hadn't noticed slide off my chest and cling to my arms, their tiny claws hooked in my shipsuit.

The majority of the sickness goes with them, the rest of it disappears as soon as my shields go up.

The critter in my hands doesn't appear sick, not really. I lift it up so I can peer into its pinprick black eyes.

'Hey little dude. What's going on?'

He *fuzzes* and reaches out to bat my nose, his paw coming away with a strand of something grey-green and... moving.

Fug.

He eats it.

I shudder. 'Dude, that can't be tasty.'

He makes no comment, contentedly munching, but that sick feeling, it's knocking at the door to my brain, not so much trying to get in as reminding me it's there. And getting stronger.

I peer closer then, noting the critter's golden fur is dull and patchy, and there's a lopsided red line around its mouth. It grows thicker on one side, expanding like a drop of water, getting shiny and round before... It dribbles down his muzzle and splats on my hand.

Blood.

I sit up. 'What the Terra?'

'Kuma Darzi, you're awake.' Ag, the sub-AI the oversees the agricultural decks, hovers above the deck at my feet, but it's not her I notice. It's the carpet of dead critters all around. A small wave of sleek golden fur. Golden balls curled around themselves, tiny paws clutching their bellies, blood staining their mouths. Some are still moving in slow, jerky motions, still more are crawling away from me. A line of critters slowly dragging themselves toward their mates, and the *fuzzing*, Old Terra, but I can sense it through the floor, in the air, and as soon as that happens I can perceive it, that knocking against my brain taking on a sharp edge of pain and darkness.

The little guy in my hand is shivering now, his pain radiating through my palm. 'What's going on? What's wrong with them?'

'When I found you, you were covered in an invasive mould. The critters are clearing the infestation. Unfortunately, the current stock are not as hardy as I hoped, but with sufficient numbers we appear to have saved you.'

Sufficient numbers.

I look out over the carpet of fuzz, at the little bodies curled in foetal balls, some still breathing, some... not. All those critters, all those lives, for me. I want to hurl, but something cold and cruel has gripped my spine, something a lot like horror.

'You are fortunate, Kuma,' Ag continues. 'My efforts to clear other areas have failed.'

Failed. That word brings to mind other swathes of dead critters, makes the cruel thing dig its claws deeper.

My hand tightens around the critter in my palm.

'How—' Horror has a hold on my throat, squeezing it so hard my voice comes out thin and broken. I try again. 'How many critters are there?'

There's something about Ag's avatar, something strange that's trying to get past the horror, something not quite *right*. I can't deal with it now though, so I push it away.

Ag cocks her head like the question confuses her. 'There are currently eleven thousand, three hundred and eighty-six units in storage and several thousand in operation. Do you wish me to deploy them?'

I shake my head. 'No, I mean...' I'm picturing Grea in her pod, p'Endr's body on the deck, the captain's hand forever reaching out of the stasis gel, and I can't help but see all the *other* bodies, gold fuzzy ones. I take a deep breath. 'No. How many critters died?'

The AI blinks and this time the confusion is written across her features. 'Since when, Kuma? My records are extensive.'

'Since the fug!'

'Eight hundred and sixty-seven thousand, five hundred and eighty-nine units have passed through Reclamation.'

'That's...' I clutch the critter to my chest. The little dude reaches for a strand of fug still clinging to my suit. I tug it out of his grip. 'That's a lot.'

'It is several years' worth of units. The Hatchery is at maximum growth capacity, but it will not be enough to fill current requirements.'

'Oh.' It seems like the thing to say, even if it doesn't seem that way. It's all that makes it around the lump of... of what? There's sludge in my chest, wrapping black tendrils around my heart, weighing it down with guilt.

I know I shouldn't be guilty. It's the critters job to look after us, to eat the junk we leave behind, our blood, sweat and vomit. Fug's one more biological for them to clean up.

Glancing over the sea of fuzzy bodies, the thought doesn't make me feel better. It makes me feel worse. If it weren't for me, they wouldn't be dead.

The little golden dude *fuzzes* against my chest, weak and thready and I know that I won't let him die.

'I need you to fix him.' I hold up Dude.

The avatar doesn't even pretend to look. 'It is a critter. It has performed its function.'

'You're still going to fix him.'

'Critters do not have genders. And no, I do not have the resources to repair the critter. If I did, I would produce units with the appropriate resistance to the...' Ag pauses a second, her face kinda scrunching up. 'The fug,' she finally says.

'Who does then?'

'Medical, but I lost contact with that sub-AI shortly after the Core went offline.'

'Okay.' I get to my feet. 'Then we'll go to Med deck.' I turn toward the lifts, stepping carefully even as I steadfastly ignore the carnage at my feet. If I look at them, if I *think* about them...

I can already hear my heart speeding up, the cold cruel thing tightening its hold on my spine. I'm going to fix Dude first and *then*, I'll deal with the others.

Ag appears in front of me. 'All access to Med deck has been terminated.'

'What? But...What do you mean, "terminated"?'

'Restricted, cut off, blocked. To reach Medical you will need to clear several sections of... fug.'

I glance down at Dude, at the stain growing around his mouth. 'He won't make it.'

'Indeed Kuma, it would be best if you—'

I turn on my heel, still careful to avoid the dead and dying littered all around me, and ignore the rest of what Ag has to say. I'm not giving up.

✳

Dude's cuddled up against my chest. The blood staining his muzzle has trickled down his chin in the minutes it takes us to reach the

Hatchery, and he's shivering.

You'd expect the Hatchery to be big, but it isn't. Not a big as the acres of Ag deck, not even as big as the lab where Dad pulls apart the molecules of alien species. It's bigger than the room I share with Grea, maybe even as big as home, which isn't that big... but yeah, not the point. The door opens and slides shut behind us, cutting off the swish and sigh of the crops, leaving us in a space not much bigger than the half of our living space that makes up the lounge. It's quiet in here. Too quiet. And clean. Critters aren't exactly messy to begin with, but the young ones tend to shed all over the place and not even the maintenance bots are able to keep on top it. A trip to the Hatchery usually means throwing my shipsuit through the cycler and making sure the nano-bots clean up every little bit of fluff before Mum puts the delicates through.

Dude shivers again, his *fuzz* taking on an ugly, metallic quality that scrapes up and down my spine.

'Okay, Dude. Maybe Ag can't make new critters resistant to the fug yet, but there's got to be something in here that can fix you. At least for the moment.'

Dude fuzzes again. It might be agreement, but he could be hungry. Or dying.

Yeah, not going there.

I put him on my shoulder, try not to wince at the sharp prick as his claws dig into the shipsuit, and head for the console in the middle of the room.

I know I said before that Hatchery isn't very big – I was kinda lying. I mean, technically, the control room *is* the Hatchery, at least that's what everyone means when they say "the Hatchery", but that's because the rest of the place, where the critters are made, isn't exactly accessible. At least not by anything bigger than a critter. Or the fug, but I'm not going there either. The control room is lit up with a soft golden light, all smooth holo-walls and white decking. Mac once said it looked like a hover-seller's showroom, sleek and clean and swish enough to convince people they needed the latest and greatest. Don't ask me how he knew that, it was one of the many strange things about Mac.

The console itself is a tiny podium in the middle of the room, a thin stick of plasform big enough to tell you where to stand. It rises out of the decking stopping when it's high enough I can touch it without having to do more than lift a finger. The room changes the moment my skin makes contact, as if it's read my mind. It hasn't. As much as some have tried, psionic communication with non-organic beings is still woo-woo crazy. Not even those fitted with greyware can really *talk* to an AI, no matter how much tech they have implanted in their brains.

Around me, the walls become transparent, showing the miniature corridors and endless grow tubes that make up the real Hatchery. Another AI appears at my side.

It's not Ag. Even if I wasn't expecting this particular avatar, I'd have known that. For one, it looks about as much like Ag as Ag looks like the Core, and for two... well the Hatchery AI isn't as extensive as Ag. It's a subset of a sub-AI, without the personality and emotion enhancements of its parent. It's got this blank, mechanical expression and flat voice that kinda freaks me out. Generally, I try to avoid it, and when I can't I try not to remember all those all old vids Mac made me watch last cycle, the ones with the Old Terra computers that went nuts and killed people.

Thankfully, Ag shivers into existence beside it. She looks kinda pissed.

She's directing most of that pissed-offness at the Hatchery avatar, staring at it like she's insulted by its existence. Frankly, if a part of me was as bland and boring as Hatch, I'd be insulted too, but I'm thankfully just me, and dealing with a boring fragment is going to be easier than Ag.

Carefully, I lift Dude from my shoulder and balance him on the platform that's appeared at the top of the console.

'Run diagnostic,' I say.

Hatch shimmers. 'Running,' it says.

Ag crosses her arms. 'I have already tried this Kuma.'

'I'm fixing Dude.'

'It is a critter. It does not need *fixing*.'

'He's ill, isn't he?'

I know I've got Ag by the logic circuits when it's face scrunches up like Grea's when she's contemplating whether or not she can get away with flushing me out an airlock. 'The resources required to heal this critter would be better applied elsewhere.'

'Medical will need something to study, to come up with a cure.'

'I have plenty of specimens—'

'But not living ones.' Not that I intend to let Medical study Dude. That particular AI made rucnarts seem warm and fuzzy.

That shuts Ag up.

The screen changes.

I'm not a medic, but the red all over the graph is bad, and the words that start coming out of Hatch's mouth aren't making me feel better.

'A high concentration of foreign bodies has compromised the integrity of the unit's molecular structure, resulting in multiple organ dysfunction.'

'Okay.' I nod like all of that didn't sound like Old Terran, familiar enough to know that is was worse than bad, but not enough to understand. 'I don't get it.'

'The...' Ag pauses for a moment, its nose screwing up like it's about to say something filthy. 'The *fug* is eating it.'

'Oh, Dude.' Dude kind of wilts on the console, his fur seeming to turn dull and limp under my eyes. 'That's bad, and kinda ironic.' I turn back to Hatch. 'Fix him,' I say.

Hatch flickers a second and the screen changes, showing DNA strands and X-rays, before it freezes.

I know without checking the logs that Ag has put the kibosh on my command.

'Kuma Darzi, I cannot—'

I put my hand up and Ag pauses mid-word. Here's the really cool thing about being crew. The AI has to do what I say. And since I'm the only crew member actually awake, well, I might as well be Captain.

'I order you to fix him.'

The Hatchery hums, the screens unfreezing and a box forms out of nowhere, enclosing Dude in a clear plasglas shell.

Really, I'm not sure why I'm so fixated on fixing a critter. Ag is right, Dude isn't anything special, in fact from his colouring, I'm pretty sure he's a generic model, one in a hundred that live and die as quickly as the air cycles through the cleaners. There'll be another thousand like him scampering out of Hatchery next week, and the week after that and the one after that. Eating and digging and whatever else they do for the next hundred years. I can't even say what it is that makes my heart clutch at the bright red blood staining his jaw or the thought of the fug eating away at his insides. Except he was on my forehead when I woke, warm and soft and *fuzzing* like he was chasing away my nightmares.

It doesn't really make sense to fix him. I shouldn't be wasting time. There are more important things I should be doing, other *sapients* I should be saving. I should be finding some way to get to the Core, or get Jim Engineer out, or Grea. But...

There was that 'but' again, the one that always got me into trouble.

Somehow, Ag has managed to deepen her glare, even though I've put her on pause. It shouldn't make me nervous, but she was so good at it that I could almost sense her anger shiver in my brain.

Which is impossible, by the way. Only biological brains can produce the particular energy required to produce a psionic signature. But still...

I clear my throat and resist the urge to scuff my boot against the deck. 'So,' I say.

Is it my imagination or does Ag glare harder?

I turn away and concentrate on Dude, pretending like I can't see the avatar out the corner of my eye. I'm really glad Hatchery isn't on an outer ring. No airlocks within easy distance.

My eyes flick up to the little slits in the bulkhead. Although, it's not like Ag couldn't seal the room and suck the oxygen out.

✳

It takes four hours, fifty-seven minutes and thirteen seconds to fix Dude. I know because I asked Hatch.

With Ag glaring at me from the corner it felt longer. I tried dismissing her at one point, but she flickered for a second and came back. Core must have really been pushing its personality matrix during the last stasis cycle, 'cause it kinda felt like having my sister over my shoulder the whole time. Ag did just enough to follow my orders before she was back to glare at me.

It freaked me out.

When Hatch finally announced Dude was done, I snatched him from the plinth and hot footed it out of there.

Unfortunately, Ag followed.

'The critter is not fully repaired.'

I'm striding down the corridor like my arse is on fire, but that stops me in my tracks. 'What?'

Ag hasn't bothered with legs, she's keeping pace with me at shoulder height and I'm totally ignoring the hint of malice in her gaze. 'I told you, Kuma. I do not have the resources to repair… fug damage.' Like before, she said "fug" like it offended her logic circuits.

Okay. Okay. Take a breath, don't panic. That brief glimpse of anger and malice, the way Ag's faced twisted up had to be a figment of my imagination. Five hours in a small room with an AI trying to glare holes in my back has obviously rattled me, 'cause the thought hovering at the back of my mind is: that's not possible.

AIs don't ignore orders because they're angry. They don't have emotions for one thing.

Still, I can't stop the words coming out of my mouth. 'What'd you do?'

Ag blinked and the confusion that rolls across her face seems so real, like she's startled by my accusation. If she'd been human, I would feel reassured. But she isn't and I swear I can sense emotion rolling in the air between us, like some kind of mirage.

Everything in me is yelling at me to run, but how do you escape from something with a response time of a fraction of a nanosecond?

You keep it busy.

I reach up, burying my fingers in Dude's fur.

'Agricultural sub-AI, I order you to run a diagnostic.'

Ag pauses, mouth open while static runs through her head.

I run.

CHAPTER EIGHT

I didn't stop running until I hit the freight lines. Except to pick up the Franken-thrower.

It was a little chewed, some of the bio-gel that connected the hard-light generator to the power-paks were broken and there were new holes in the grip, but I grabbed it anyway. Okay, so there was also that side trip to a maintenance locker, and maybe I took a few minutes to grab a bag and raid some of the freight containers piled up in the station. A guy had to eat, and there was no way I was going up against the fug again without something to protect me from the screeching. After all, it was the screeching that got me in the first place. And maybe the soot. But whatever.

I had food, earmuffs and an enviromask when I went back into the speedway.

I forgot water though. I realised this two seconds ago, about the same time I stopped running.

My mouth isn't dry exactly, but there's that foul, filmy kinda taste on my tongue, like you get when you've been running from a crazy sub-AI and you forgot to grab water while you were stuffing your bag full of supplies.

A part of me thinks I'm crazy for thinking that Ag is crazy. AIs don't do crazy. At least, they're not meant to. I heard this rumour once that one of the reasons the war started was because an old AI lost its shit. Some kind of programming error or something that made it release the Regan virus. You know, the one that turned all the straight, full-humans into hybrids? It was a big deal.

Of course, it was a rumour. The AI got blown up, its processing core destroyed by the Regan herself. That was an even *bigger* deal. One no one really wanted to know about. According to everyone who remembers anything about the war, the Regan was scary shit.

I wonder what she would do if it were her here and not me.

It's not like I can blow up the Core, or even Ag's processing core. For all I know, Core's fine, holed up behind its energy shield, and I could have imagined the malice in Ag's gaze, the confusion that coated the air between us. I *could* have imagined it. The part of me that doesn't think I'm crazy though? That part of me is shit scared. That part is urging me to get up and keep running, to get away from the Ag decks as fast as I can. It doesn't care that my mouth is a desert and sweat has stuck my shipsuit to my back, or that there's a stitch cramping up the whole left side of my ribs, or my legs are mush from running.

It knows what it saw, what it felt, impossible though it is. AIs aren't meant to *feel*; not like that, no matter how experimental their programming. But mould isn't meant to eat a ship either, isn't meant to chase rucnarts through the Aer, isn't meant to bite. The fug has done crazy shit to the ship, maybe its infected Ag too. Maybe that's why Core cut itself off. But if that's the case, if the rest of the ship is infected and the captain's dead and Jim Engineer is stuck in his pod...

My heart's running like *I'm* still running; big, heavy thumps in my chest.

This isn't good. This is so far from good it's in another solar system.

Panic is blooming, spreading over my chest in a hot steady stream of "get up and run".

Right now, running's a good survival strategy.

I'm on my feet, pushing off the side of the freight tube and stumbling into an uncoordinated jog. My feet aren't moving like they should, my knees, my thighs, all of it's jelly, but the steady stream of panic is a steady hand at my back.

Panic's an ugly emotion. Take it from an empath. It's like fear, except fear doesn't grab hold of your brain and make you do stupid shit. Doesn't make you forget about the Franken-thrower over your shoulder or ignore the steadily growing hum of the mag-lines.

Panic gums up your senses until you're blind, deaf and dumb, too addled to even see the fug before you run into it.

And as much as I know all that, as much as I've fought against it in other minds, as much as I know that I have to stop, have to take a breath and use my brain, I can't. P'Endr, Grea, and the captain, they're all jumbled up in my head, dying, yelling, reaching for me with clawed, bloated hands.

All the fear, all the worry, all the nightmares I've been holding back since Onah pushed me out of stasis/sleep... It's cracked the dam I hid it behind and now I'm drowning in it. In nightmares. In everything I ever feared and a few things I didn't know I *had* to fear.

I'm alone. All alone. In the dark and cold. In the void. And all the things, all the people who promised to keep me safe – Mum, Dad, the captain and Jim Engineer – they're not here to save me.

I don't know what to do.

It's Dude that saves me. He keeps the panic back enough that when the first bit of fug gets me, tugs on my arm and spins me around, I recognise the palette rushing toward me, taking up all the space.

Panic can be useful. Not always, but sometimes. It floods your system with adrenalin, and if you can keep enough of your mind to use it, it makes leaping out the way of speeding death really easy.

I'm flattened against the bulkhead, belly to the steelcrete, holding on like my palms grew suckers, feeling the whoosh of air like a razor blade against my spine.

Some part of me can still reason, which is probably why I'm still breathing after the palette zooms past.

Everyone will tell you that critters aren't hunters, not intelligent enough, too submissive, bred to obey not think. We've been testing them on the wrong things. In that moment where I'm forced to stillness, to concentrate on the death scraping my spine, Dude pounces. Not physically, not like a rucnart or a qwan, not even like Grea on something she thought she could blame on me. Nope, he pounces on my fear, his *fuzz* swallowing it, pushing out panic and doubt until all that's left is that soft gold glow.

A weight's lifted from my shoulders. It makes me giddy. It's lucky there are no other palettes following the first or they'd clean me up as I stumble away from the bulkhead.

Giddiness is almost as bad as panic, or at least that's what Dude must assume, because the glow retreats a little, enough to see the fug.

Really see it.

'Oh shit.'

See, this is why panic is bad. And probably giddiness as well.

Somewhere along the line, the bulkheads had turned from off-white to a grey-green carpet of moving, growing mould. Tendrils hang from the ceiling, reaching toward me, growing. And I hadn't noticed.

Dude *fuzzes* against my neck again and moves, scuttling after a patch of grey-green wrapped around my arm. I rip it off before he reaches my shoulder, brush off the stuff on my chest, out of my hair. There's a bit of panic in all those movements, making them rough and quick and almost frenzied. I don't know whether the panic comes from the thought of the fug eating Dude or Dude eating the fug. Probably both. But I just got Dude fixed, however temporary that might be, and there's no way I'm losing him.

No. Way.

Once it's let loose, panic never really goes away, but you can mask it, can push it back, use it to keep you moving forward. Inside his bubble of calm, Dude's given me a moment to reason, to act instead of reacting; to regain a tiny semblance of control. To remember the Franken-thrower, the enviro-mask in my stolen bag and my mission.

I'm going to save Dude, engineer a new breed of fug-proof critters and lord it over my sister until the end of the universe. I slide the enviro-mask into place, pull on the earmuffs, and heft the Franken.

But first, I've got some burning to do.

The Franken-thrower is hot, even through the gloves, but I don't stop burning. Not for a nano-second.

Dude's a warm, comforting weight on my shoulder, and as I burn, I imagine the two of us standing in the middle of the freight line like we're in one of those old vids. Faces protected by dark faceplates, necks covered in soot as I lay waste to the fug. It'd be pretty cool, except for the pink camo, and maybe the gunk in my hair. If Grea were here, she'd have remembered to switch her shipsuit to some kind of sleek black-on-black pattern and found some of those chunky, Old Terra-style boots from somewhere, the kind that went all the way up to her knees. And she'd have saved p'Endr, and the rucnart would be there too, snarling at the fug even as a horde of critters flowed around her feet, attacking the mould.

Grief wells in my chest, trying to push its way up my throat and blind me with tears. I push the daydream aside and concentrate on the Franken-thrower, on the heat of the barrel and its red path of destruction.

Smoke pours off the web, the fug curling up and dying, leaving a fine trail of soot on the decking. It's screaming. The earmuffs muffle the worst of it, but there's still this insane, high-pitched whine that gets through. I tried blasting some music, something loud and heavy the last user had downloaded from the archives, but not even Old Terran rock can drown fug.

There's a hatch up ahead, hidden by the retreating vines. A few more metres and I'll be there, wherever there is. The fug makes everything appear different, and without a map or AI to guide me, I'm pretty sure I got lost somewhere in the maintenance tubes. With all of the backtracking and climbing, trying to find a clear path between Ag and Med, it's a wonder I didn't end up in the ice hull.

Citlali is not-quite egg-shaped, squashed on top and not so much on the bottom.

Stasis was in the vertical middle, and somehow, after my first encounter with the fug, Ag had whisked me down three decks to Ag. That meant I had to go up. Way up. Med was above Stasis, along with Command and Operations.

It was in the middle of the ship, the safest place. Or, you know, so everyone thought. I bet Lyn Captain wouldn't think that way anymore, if she still could.

I'd stopped trying to figure out how the fug had known to hit the middle of the ship about three seconds after I'd stopped worrying about how it did anything. Which was half a cycle after I encountered the first blockage in the freight lines. I don't even know how to describe it. "A mess" didn't quite cover the chaos of palettes jammed up in the tubes. It looked like one had broken down and others had rammed into the back of it, sending crates and plasteel flying everywhere. Some of the palettes must have been going really fast, launching themselves over the others crashing through the bulkhead, adding biogel and bright sparks of raw power to the mess.

Some of the crates had split apart, spilling grain and food all over the tube. The fug had covered it all, making its own little eco-system, feeding on the plasform and steelcrete. It was as much like a jungle as I'd ever seen. The carpet of mould was so thick it could have been grass, and the tendrils that had assaulted me in the maintenance tube were broad enough they could have been trees. If trees grew from the ceiling and walls, sprouting prehensile branches that wound through the holes the mould had made in crates and palettes alike, ripping steelcrete and plasform apart like it was... I don't know. Old Terra paper maybe?

I'd turned the Franken on the creepy jungle, pushing the heat up high.

Even through the ear muffs the screaming had just about taken me to my knees. Turns out, the thicker the fug, the harder it was to kill.

Some of it had broken off and come for me like it had legs.

I hadn't thought the stuff could move that fast, but still, I'd stood my ground and hit it with the Franken.

Only Dude bitting my chin had saved me from becoming fug food.

That had been the start of my epic journey to everywhere but where I wanted to go. The fug had blocked off everything that lead directly to Med, and the closer I got to the Core, the worse it became.

I don't know how long it's taken me to get here, but the bag full of supplies is lighter than when I started and I'm really starting to wish I had stims to keep me awake. Adrenalin and cold have kept me going until now, but my eyes are getting heavy and not even the daydream of how cool Dude and I would be in an Old Terran vid is enough to stop the desperate need for sleep. That hatch is what's keeping me going, that and the slowly clearing path to it. I may not know *exactly* where we are, but I know we're above Stasis, above the choking jungles of fug and that's good enough for me.

Maybe the fug senses the hatch is all that's keeping me going, because it redoubles its efforts. A huge tendril bursts from a crack in the bulkhead, slapping and whipping around. I duck, not quite fast enough and it smacks me in the head, throwing me against the wall before it comes at me again.

I roll to my feet and out of the way, right into a thick patch of fug. I try to scramble back, to bring the Franken up and blast it, but the fucking tendril is everywhere, snapping like it wished it had teeth.

Dude's still on my shoulder. The little guy must have claws of plasteel, 'cause I don't know how he's holding on as I duck and weave and try not to fall on my arse. At least he's not going for the fug wriggling up my shoulder. We came to some kind of agreement along the way. He didn't eat fug and I didn't freak out. It seemed reasonable at the time. Doesn't stop him from giving me a heart attack though. Like now. He dashes for the fug, and I ignore the tendril for a second, ripping the mould off my shipsuit.

A second is all the fug needs to strike.

Something hits me from behind.

The Franken falls from my grip and skitters across the deck. Dude goes with it, not even his wicked little claws enough to keep him attached as I go flying.

Right into the fug.

Not the blackened, retreating carpet of the stuff either, but the deep, thick, viscous crap.

My heart's got enough time to squeeze before I hit the deck on my belly.

Air bursts out of my lungs. My vision goes white and for a second I forget where I am.

It's like coming out of stasis all over again, except this time, when my vision clears, there's no decking, no AI to remind me to breathe. Just fug. In my face.

I'd rather be staring down a rucnart.

Everything goes still.

The stuff's got no eyes and yet it's staring at me. I don't know how, but I can sense it. A sweet spot of tension between my shoulder blades, and I know that it's waiting for me to make the first move before it pounces.

The Franken's there, a lunge and a shuffle from the tips of my fingers and Dude's sitting on top of it, like an island in the middle of a volcano. He's not moving either, and I imagine, if this were a vid, he'd be standing on one paw with little swords in his hands, snarling at the mould.

I shake the image off. I need to get out of here, and I'm not leaving Dude.

What's the fug waiting for?

There's a grey-green shadow in the corner of my eye. I can't quite make it out but it's long and thin and it looks a lot like the tendril that was smacking me around. I have the sense that it's growing, or maybe that's because it's getting closer, sneaking over my head for a kill shot. Dude's glaring at it, his little body tensing, his fur sleeking out, his tiny muzzle wrinkling, lips pulling back over sharp, sharp teeth. And it's like, holy Terra, there's a miniature rucnart crouched atop the Franken, and I swear, I *swear* that's an *emote* coming off him in a spine-curdling blast of menace.

For just a second, the fug pulls back.

That's it. I lunge. One hand propelling me forward, the other reaching for the Franken.

The fug attacks.

My hand closes over the plasform. Dude's climbing up my wrist and it's like I have eyes in the back of my head. I see the grey-green shadow aiming for my back, its sharp, spear-like tip going for my heart.

Roll. Point. Shoot.

The fug's screaming again, the stuff that's not clinging to my shipsuit. There's no time to rip it off. I'm in the middle of the shit now. Green at my feet, new tendrils breaking out of the freight tube, cracking the steelcrete, ripping out of holes. All of them coming for me.

Point. Shoot.

I spin, searching for the hatch.

There.

I guess getting thrown into the fug was both good and bad. The hatch is a few steps away, and now that I'm in the thick of it, I'm not worrying too much about not stepping on fug. The faster I move, the harder I am to catch.

One step. Two.

Burn fug, burn.

The fug's eaten the control panel. But really, what else did I expect? It's fug.

There's not much left of the panel, a few bits of biogel and a nub of plasform to show where it once was.

The fug hasn't gotten as far with the hatch itself. Either the steelcrete here is thicker, or the fug's got better things to do, 'cause there are only a few shallow pock marks in its surface. Which, I hope, means it hasn't got to Medical yet (or wherever I am). Of course, that also leaves me with a problem. How to get through the hatch.

I need another pair of hands, someone to hold off the fug while I search for a way in. But it's only Dude and me, and Dude's not big enough to hold the Franken.

I'm gonna have to be quick—

Rage. It hits me under the ribcage. Bloodlust follows it, a sucker-punch to the jaw, and for a second my vision goes red, and I can taste something strange on my tongue, something musty and sour. I want... I want...

Violence.

To tear with teeth and claws, to rip into the enemy and feast—

I shut the foreign *emote* out. Shake the red from my vision and try not to let shock slow me down. There's a golden fuzz to the *emote*, and even if it hadn't been emanating from my shoulder, I'd have known who was pushing it. Dude's got some serious clout for a creature the size of both my fists. I want to know how he's doing it, but there's no time. No time for anything except to rip the fug off the bulkhead and pray for an emergency release, and hope even harder the panel isn't as fucked as the ones on Stasis.

Something must be smiling on me because it works. The fug's even been useful for a change. The steelcrete covering the emergency release is gone save for a thin honeycomb of metal. I punch through it. The latch is a little corroded, but it doesn't shatter when I throw my weight against it.

For a second, nothing happens. I push harder, hear something crack, try not to imagine the handle snapping even as the steelcrete crumbles under my hand.

And then I'm stumbling forward, half the latch in my hand, but not caring because the hatch is rolling open and I'm diving through it, the Franken slung over my shoulder, Dude still *emoting* on my shoulder.

The hatch snaps shut.

CHAPTER NINE

I'm not on Medical. I'm on Lab Two, two decks above Medical.

I guess I got *really* turned around in the freight tubes.

After I shut the hatch, all the fear and adrenaline that had been keeping me going, left in a rush. I had enough energy to get to my feet, strip the fug from my clothes and burn it with the Franken, before stumbling to the nearest lab.

Sleep's pulling at my bones, making my eyes cross. It's only the cold keeping me awake.

The life-support on this deck is toast, and not the good kind where the butter's melting into the crumb. It's the bad kind, the kind where I'm pretty sure Dude and I are the only things generating heat, and he's too small to do more than keep the frostbite out of my fingers. But there's stuff in the lab I find, a whole back wall full of junk the last occupant hasn't gotten around to throwing in the cyclers.

I crank the thermal layer in my shipsuit all the way up before sorting through the junk. It's not much. I mean there's a *lot* of junk, but the old test tubes won't do much to keep us warm and of the stuff that will, we'll make do.

I use a cutter to chop up a few of the workbenches and make a kind of hut in the corner. Just three sides and bit of plasform on top to help hold in the heat. A few old scraps of shipsuit go on the floor and some thick, squiggly stuff that might have been plasform (if someone stuffed it in a microwave) wraps around the inside. The resulting space is small, enough for me to huddle up with Dude against my chest, but that's the point.

If the fug finds us, I'm banking of Dude warning me before it gets close enough to eat me.

I sleep on the floor, head on my pack, Dude cuddled up under my chin. He'd still *emoting* when I close my eyes, the same anger and bloodlust as in the tubes, but lessened. It was comforting in its own weird way.

In the seconds before sleep takes me, I wonder at that. I've never spent this much time with a critter, but the things I've seen him do and the *emoting* aren't something I thought a critter was capable of. They're a little bit psionic, enough for the kin to rearrange their thought patterns, but they're not that bright. Or are they? I mean, the rucnarts have to have something to work with, you can't get an animal to do something if it's stone cold stupid. At least, that's what I've been told. Maybe I should ask them.

I hadn't meant to do more than sleep, but after a nightmare where I ran through stone corridors, shadows moving like snakes on the walls and silver lightning nipping at my heels, I slipped into the Aer.

The Aer isn't like what Jørgens experience in stasis/sleep. I mean, it could be, if we all got together and created our own little world. And sometimes a few of us do, mucking around in each other's memories. It's something to kill the time. But we don't do things like the kin. *No one* does things like the kin.

Stepping into the Aer isn't easy, or it shouldn't be. There's a wall between Jørgens and kin, not a natural one, but something the Jørans made.

I press my hand to it, sensing the way it wobbles and bounces at my touch, the static charge that runs up my arm. It's a warning. There are teeth in the wall, and claws and fangs. All sorts of nasty, pain-filled things designed to keep nosey human half-breeds out. The qwans don't say it like that, but the rucnarts do. All of us have slipped into the Aer at some point, we're nosey half-breeds after all, but most of us usually only try it once. The teeth and the claws and all that.

But not me. And not Grea. I guess it's part of being an empath, and why the kin don't like us so much. Their defences kinda slide right over us. All that buzzing, tingling sensation ripping up and down my arm feels like it's trying to chew through a layer of air above my skin. The teeth and claws graze my arms and neck, but nothing catches flesh.

I push through the wall.

For a moment, I'm under water, staring up at the sun, a million flesh-eating piranhas swirling around me in whirlpools of frustrated rage. It's one of those moments that stretch and stretch, seeming to spread into eternity, and no matter how hard you kick or claw your way upwards, the surface is always out of reach.

This is where most first-timers freak out and bail. Even Mac. But not me, and not Grea.

When it's like the air is going to burn in my lungs, I take a deep breath and step sideways.

The Aer spreads before me and it's wrong.

For one, Dude's on my shoulder. I want to wonder how he got there, I mean, not on my shoulder, but on my shoulder on the psionic plane, but have to add it to the list of weird shit about him and move on. There's no time to ponder it now.

I'm standing on a wide, sun-scorched plain under a sky so blue it hurts to look at. The soil under my feet is red as blood. It puffs and swirls around my boots with every step, carrying with it an iron tang of fear and something else, something that slithers up my spine and lodges in my throat.

I need fangs. That thought is strange but it sticks in the back of my head and refuses to let go. I try to shake it off, to pry it from my skull, digging my fingers into the thick goop and yanking, but all that does is make it cling tighter. All I come away with is some multicoloured crap that sticks under my fingernails and stinks like old socks and panic.

Shit. I know what this is.

It's the rainbow running through the goop that gives it away. Training memories. I'm stuck in a training memory. The goop sliding over my skull is a psionic history lesson. Forget vids, tutors, or the old timers telling you how it was back in the day, this wasn't merely history inserted into your brain, this was the *memory* of someone who'd been there when shit got real. Although judging from the kaleidoscope turning this memory white, it wasn't just *one* memory.

Double shit. Multi-memory trainings were the *worst*, and this one felt new, stickier than the others I'd encountered, raw like it wasn't so much a trainer as a nightmare. As if whomever the memories came from was reliving the experience without the dulling passage of time, or the blurring effect of passing through generations of minds.

I know without trying that it's not going to let go.

If my empathic abilities hadn't been stronger than my minuscule telepathic ones, the memory would have caught me up in a red-hot second. As it was…

The goop's sliding over my fingers and I can feel it tricking over my forehead and dripping onto my nose.

Sighing, I pluck Dude from my shoulder and put him on the red dirt at my feet. There's no need for both of us to get caught up in this.

'Don't get lost,' I tell him before I let the training memories take over.

I'm still on the red plain, but it's no longer empty, no longer silent.

The ground shakes as shuttles roar overhead, while the snap of weapons fire reverberates in my ears and snarls rip through the air, raising the gooseflesh on my arms. It's the screams that shiver across my flesh though, that make my heart leap to my throat and stop it with fear. They rise high and piercing and then stop, cut off on a wet gurgle.

The ground is red with more than sand.

There's a dome in the distance, the size of a dozen shuttles, its roof shredded, bits of plasform flapping in the wind, the shattered remnants of supporting rods scattered over the ground. Around it are bodies – human and rucnart. In the peculiar way of the eter, one moment I'm standing atop a rock, far enough from the battlefield that the figures might as well be nanites and the next I'm in the midst of it. There's a wounded qwan at my feet, a trio of rucnarts standing over it, snouts bloody and fangs bared. Not even a metre away, a human in an envirosuit gasps, blood bubbling from his lips and pouring from the wounds on his chest.

All around me there is carnage, blood, death. Rage. So much rage it rises from the ground and curls around my knees, tugging on my shipsuit, clawing at my shields.

Then nothing.

Fear slithers up my spine, turns me around even through everything in me is yelling at me to run. To run and never look back.

A woman stands on the outskirts of the carnage. Short and dark, her eyes like pitiless pools, blood and loss and rage distorting her face. Ice forms in the pit of my stomach. I am a hundred rucnarts all at once, a dozen qwans. We could fall on her in a second, sink talons and fangs into soft human flesh and tear her apart as we have the others, and yet…

And yet…

Power whips around her; dark chocolate swirls laced with blue lightning and now she is the size of a mountain, as endless as the sea.

I know her, know her like I know the fug that chases me through my nightmares, that stops my heart in my chest, but her name is lost in the flash of terror, of dread as she raises her arms and—

I tear myself out of the memory breathing hard, hands on knees, heart trying to rip its way out of my chest.

Old holy Terran shit.

The Regan. That was *the* Regan.

Fuck. If that was what she'd been like in real life, no wonder she single-handedly stopped the war.

Citlali was being eaten by hyperactive mould and the Jørans were having nightmares about the final days of the war. What was up with that? My dreams are full of fug; I'm as sure of that as I am grateful that I don't remember them. So why are the Jørans focused on something that happened a century ago?

Unless...

I dip back into the memory. Not the training memory, but *my* memory. I don't want to get caught in whatever horror the Jørans are reliving – the first time was bad enough.

Overhead, the shuttles roar. I pause it and, instead of looking out at the carnage on the plain, I turn my gaze up. The shuttles are big, sleek machines with patterns carved into their sides and silver-black hulls. And they're not human-made. Not. Human. Made.

A lodestone hits the bottom of my gut.

That...

Brain reset. A few blank seconds where I try to fit the implications of that into my worldview. Twisting and turning the image above me, trying to find a space in everything I know for it to fit, and then, when I do.

'Old Terra...'

Except it's not Old Terran, that image. It's something else, an echo from the ancient past and a shadow of the war that created the Regan.

The Regan.

I bring that memory up, make it hover on the sand in front of me, the shuttle casting her in darkness. Even in the snapshot I've drawn out of the memory, the lightning in her hands snaps and spits, like not even a hundred years and the cast of a hundred minds can contain the power under her skin. Stepping closer makes my flesh crawl. She was meant to be ferocious, to be a force unlike any the world had ever faced. I'd learned her name in class, but it never stuck, only her title, and the fear it brought to people's minds. A yellow wave rippled with the sparkle of awe.

She doesn't look like I remember from the vids, but that's not unusual, memory warps features all the time, makes her teeth a little sharper, her eyes a little darker. Besides, it's not her face that tickles my awareness, the sense of something not right is coming from elsewhere. I peer closer, circling her, trying to find the niggle burrowing under my skin. The lightning makes it harder, constantly distracting me, drawing my eyes away from her feet, her clothes.

The lightning.

There's something in the lightning, a flicker, a hint of red that doesn't belong.

I reach for it.

The ground bucks, disrupting the memory. The Regan dissipates, shredding on a non-existent breeze as the space around me changes.

I scoop Dude up as the red soil turns to snow. Massive ice-covered trees shoot up around me, branches lacing together, forming icicles like spear points aimed at my head. I can see another memory gathering, another human-shaped shadow forming next to me and I know I have to get out.

Whatever's happening with the rucnarts, it's bad enough that they've lost control of the Aer. I'm not hanging around to find out what that's like.

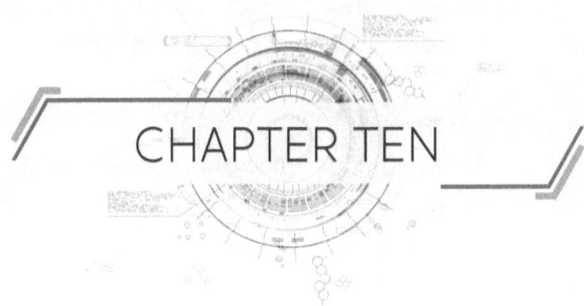

CHAPTER TEN

Eventually, I find the forest, the space where p'Endr showed me her memory. It's different. Quiet as the void. It doesn't appear as it did in the brief glimpse I had as she tried to outrun the writhing fug.

It's... fractured, and the big black sphere that hovered over it all is gone, hidden behind the dirty-grey mist that covers the valley. As I walk under the canopy, the grass cracks and pops like it's made of brittle plasform. And the air... I take deep a breath, trying to sort out the smell. There's a thick, musty scent on it, like a cut strapple left too long on the bench, the pale green flesh turned brown. But that's not all. There's something else in the air, a scent that's not so much a smell but a sense, a curdling in my gut that has nothing to do with the silence ringing in my ears.

I stop. Feet still, heart hammering. That smell/scent is beyond wrong. It makes me want to puke and then run and then puke some more.

I hunch over, hands on my knees, spit collecting in my mouth as I fight the urge. It takes more effort than it should. My knees are shaking, my knuckles white and my face is clammy with sweat and nerves. Every fibre of my being is telling me to yell "fuck it" and bolt, to rip myself out of the forest and never come back. It *hurts* to stand here, to hold onto the Aer. It hurts so bad.

It's never hurt this much before.

Why does it hurt?

I can't hold on, but I can't let go. I have to find out what's wrong with the Aer, have to talk to Onah. But my insides seem like they're going to split molecule by molecule and for a moment, as I stare at my hands on my knees, I can *see* myself drifting apart, my skin turning to dust.

I can't hold on.

Warmth spreads through my cheek on a gentle, golden *fuzz*. It spreads through my skin, easing the ache in my spine and untwisting the knot in my gut. The sick scent/sense fades, fleeing before the wave of gold, leaving my head clear enough to figure shit out.

I snap my shields up.

The pain vanishes, and the pale gold dust that was my hands snaps back, becoming flesh in the blink of an eye.

I straighten.

Fuck. What *was* that? I already know what the *fuzz* was. Dude is on my shoulder, tucked up against my ear.

Even with my shields up, the scent/sense is sneaking up on me. The only difference is I can see it now. It's the fug, writhing over grass and trees like the particularly ugly parasite it is. It's pooled at my feet, stretching upwards as it tries to find a way through the thin skin of my shield. It burns where it touches, not a hot, immediate burn, where you snatch your hand away from the cooker, but a slower, colder burn, like what I felt next to the ice hull.

There are holes in my defences where it's crept up on me and slipped through my shields, but I know what it's up to now. It won't get me again.

I crouch, snapping a tendril of fug off the carpet at my feet.

How'd it get on the psionic plane? I guess I should have wondered that when I saw p'Endr's memories, but I was too busy then, too distracted by the dying, so I'll do it now.

I'd felt something from the fug before, in the maintenance tunnel. A presence that was there and not, like it was too far away, or too small for me to sense. But how'd it get *here*?

Just because something is psionic doesn't mean it can access the

Aer. I mean, except Dude, who clearly isn't following the rules.

I shouldn't be here. The qwans make sure of that, and the rucnarts enforce the rule. But here I am, and here is the fug (and Dude, but we're worrying about him later). I'm easy to explain. The Jørans aren't here to keep me out, and well, I'm sneaky. And determined. And maybe a little nuts. But the fug?

I remember p'Endr's dying memories, the fug sweeping across the forest, wrapping her in a cocoon of evil. The fug had gotten into the Aer *while* the rucnarts were still patrolling the edges, when the qwans' defences should have been at their strongest. How had it gotten in? *Why* had it gotten in?

The fug was eating the ship, was it eating the psions too? It wasn't like you could *eat* psionic energy. Was it? Was the fug some kind of thought-eating mould? But then what would it want with steelcrete and biogel?

None of this makes sense, like it doesn't make sense for the *Citlali* to stop in the middle of interstellar space. There is nothing in the space between solar systems, that is why it's called the void. The big black. The space where parents threaten to throw little boys when they don't make their bed.

The piece of fug curls and waves in my grip, lengthening to twirl around my wrist. The rest of it gathers at my feet, wisps of vapour rising from my shields where they try to burn through. I never actually studied the fug before. I'd always been killing it or ripping it off my face, but now I have it at my feet, trapped beyond my shields. If I'm ever going to get a chance to figure the stuff out, this is it.

I sit, folding my legs under me and planting my butt on the forest floor. I push the crackle of leaves and the damp scent of moss aside, concentrating on the mould until the rest falls away. The mould is curled tight around my wrist, like an Old Terra snake trying to cut off my hand. Amongst all the dull grey and green is a sparkle, a bright pop of red like blood, if blood can glimmer. It isn't much, and it disappears if I look at it too hard.

There's something *in* it, something more than the sparkle teasing the corner of my eye. I bring it closer, narrowing my focus, making that little pop of red the only thing I see. Ditching the murky smell of fug, the vapour rising off my shields, the grey-green tendril, leaving the red nowhere to hide. It isn't as easy as it sounds. The red fights me, pulls shadows over itself and burrows deeper into the surrounding fug. The grey-green gets in on the action too, climbing up my shields, twining around my torso, growing tendrils until they reach over my head, waving and burning.

But if there is one thing I can do really well, it's focus; focus so hard that the beat of my heart falls away and I forget to breathe. The fug doesn't stand a chance.

Eventually the Aer falls away, leaving me and the red standing in a vast white space. The older Jørgens used to call it the void, that place where we go when we leave our bodies behind to concentrate on the psionic, but when you spend your life in the black of space, "void" doesn't seem like the right kind of word for the place in our heads. Somewhere along the line, we started calling it the eter. It's meant to mean something in one of the Old Terran dialects.

The eter is a big white space on the psionic plane, formless until someone like me starts playing with it. It's kinda like a holowall before Grea gets through with it. Once she does, there's a whole new world on it, full of sound and colour. That's what the eter is like, and right now it spreads around me, endless and empty, except for me and the red.

The red's bigger now, it's given up hiding. No longer a thin ribbon of blood wrapped around my fingers, but a cloud floating in front of my face. It's a ball of mist, thin at the edges and thick in the middle. It pulses, flashes of light streaking through its core, almost like it's reasoning. There's nothing coming off it though, no emotion, no thought, no bright puddles of curiosity or halos of fear. Nothing. And yet, it tried to hide.

I circle it slowly, then over it and under it, in that physics-defying way only possible in the eter. It's the same on all sides. Flashes of light, like lightning, in a ball of red mist.

I look closer, making myself smaller, trying to peer through the outer layers, to see what makes it tick. The eter turns pink as I sink deeper into the mist. It's not until I'm deep inside, the red wrapping around me like a creepy eter, that I sense anything. It inches up on me slowly, a tingle down my spine, a fizz in my fingertips. There's no colour to it, no emotion, and it's almost too late by the time I notice the presence. The mist has changed, grown thicker and solid. One moment I'm gliding through it, focused on the lightning at its centre, and then I'm caught, trapped in a solid mass of red. I try to lift my feet, but no matter how I tug or twist, they're not going anywhere. The mist travels upwards, wrapping me up like nanites in plasform. And now that I'm studying it, I can see it gathering around my knees, getting thicker and thicker until it's no longer mist. And if I *really* look, it glimmers with tiny sparks of light full of intention and... I don't know. There's still no emotion for me to pick up. The mist appears empty, and yet it can't be, because it's doing stuff. Planning. Hunting. That takes more intelligence than your average mould is capable of, even the steelcrete-eating kind.

Whatever this stuff is, whatever intelligence drives it, I can't see it. It's hiding itself somehow, pretending. Grea will tell you there's something wrong with me, a defective gene that sees something that wants to eat me and decides to fuck with it.

The mist is no exception, and the fact it's being sneaky makes me want to screw with it more.

Being trapped doesn't bother me. I mean, it would, if I wasn't in *my* eter, but I brought the red into my mind, and here I make the rules. I let it continue to slither over me, wriggling up my chest and over my head. I can see it better now. It thinks it's winning and so it's not hiding itself. The lightning is stronger and more frequent. There's still no emotion in it, nothing beyond that sliver of intent, but there's something buried in the lightning, a glimmer within the glimmer. I filter out the mist, concentrating on the lightning.

I'm pretty sure it was waiting for me to do that.

The lightning explodes.

I'm not trapped anymore, which is not as good as it sounds. My arms and legs might be my own, but the lightning has turned into a raging river in the midst of a maelstrom and I'm rocketing down it, surrounded in silver and blinding flashes of light.

I can't stop it. I'm in *my* eter. Freezing the maelstrom should be easier than breathing and yet...

And yet...

There's a sense, an uneasy shift in the space around me, like the fabric of everything is splitting and I'm about to slip through the threads of reality to see something impossible, and if I can do that, *survive* that, I'll know everything.

Everything.

I stop struggling—

I'm yanked out. Out of the river and out of the changing eter.

It shouldn't be possible. I mean, it might have been warped but it was *my* eter, my space, my world. Mine.

And yet, here I am. Not in my eter.

I should really stop expecting the possible.

I'm in somebody's eter, that much I can tell. It's more than the darkness, the cold that bites at my nose. It's the ground under my feet, the smell of roses and the musk of feathers in the air. It's a bone-deep sense of not being *me*. Yeah, and I know that sounds weird and screwy, because of course I'm me, I'm just not *in* me anymore. And that's weird.

Not weird because I've never been in someone else's eter before, but weird because this feels too... I don't know, personal I guess, like I'm sitting in someone's bathroom while they're taking a piss kind of personal. It's uncomfortable and I'm glad it's dark, because I don't want to see what's going on in the space around me. Whatever I'd see out there, it'd be more than someone's pants around their ankles.

I clear my throat. 'Hello?'

The darkness absorbs my voice, and somewhere, something ripples in response.

I try again. 'Umm, why'd you bring me here? I mean, thanks, I guess, but... ugh, you brought me in past your shields and all.'

The ripple moves through the space under my feet, and I sense more than see a shadow rise in front of me.

It is protected. The white/black voice is inaudible even in the eter. Instead the words reach out and sink into my skin, like light.

'Onah?'

There is not much time.

'Time for what?'

They will breach the engine containment soon. You must stop them.

'The fug? I'm trying, but it's like *eating* shit and the critters can't stop it and the AI is screwed and I can't wake anyone!'

No, you must stop them.

"Them" is not a word, it's a memory and it comes out of nowhere, hitting me in the forehead and swallowing me whole.

It's not like the memory of the Regan. It's old and tattered, with the imprint of a million different minds embedded in the fabric. A teaching memory, one shared and passed down from parent to chick over and again, until the mind it originally came from is lost in a storm of colour.

Pain comes. Crippling pain. It consumes my arm, my chest, the right side of my face in fire. I scream, the sound high and piercing. It comes out not human, but the shrilling cry of a qwan.

The pain is not mine. Not *mine*. I chant it until I believe it, until the burning recedes and other senses began to take over.

Smell is first, the charred scent of burnt feathers and the iron tang of blood, then sight. Giant trees crashing to the forest floor, trunks a dozen wingspans wide falling through the green, taking others with them. Branches as thick as a rucnart snapping, trunks breaking. The *BOOM* as they hit the ground, vibrating through my feet, through my bones, the screech of the birds and the scream of chicks.

Grief wails through me, rips my heart to shreds, leaving nothing but rage behind.

The scene changes, the perspective with it. I'm no longer seeing through the eyes of a qwan but down the sharp snout of a rucnart as they rip the throat from something... alien.

Its blood has the rich tang of iron, stains the creature's soft white fur a blazing red. It falls backwards under the rucnart's weight, two thick arms straining to hold the rucnart's jaws away from its neck, while two more try to staunch the flow of blood. But while the creature holds the jaws from its neck, the rucnart's claws shred the stiff fabric of its clothes.

The memory changes again and I'm running down wide curved halls, my snout and claws stained red, the musty metallic scent of the invaders thick in my nose, bloodlust and rage gripping my insides as I hunt them through their under-mountain home.

The hunt and the blood go on forever. I chase the creatures, ripping and tearing their pale flesh. They fall in endless waves. Some fight back, raising weapons that spit bolts of light. They die first. But for as many that fall to the kin's teeth and claws, more escape, fleeing in machines that roar as they dart into the sky.

The water-kin come then. Not one or two, or even a thousand. *All* of them come, joined together in the blazing, crushing light of a single mind.

There is no perspective from the swatai. Their training memories are too big, too dangerous to be held in a single mind. There is only the sense of them, an entity so big, so powerful that it can wrap around the world and crush an entire species.

The invaders that don't vanish into the sky, the ones that haven't fallen before the kin of tree and air, scream before they die. Webbed hands clutching their heads, blood running from their wide, flat noes.

Everything that makes them *Them* bursting out of their heads and flowing—

Blackness, a bit of the memory snipped away before I can see it, and then I'm back in the midst of the it and *They* are gone.

Gone from the earth, the forests, the mountains. Gone from the skies, the oceans. Gone from the endless black beyond the sky.

Just.

Gone.

The memory ends. I blink, coming back to the darkness, to the weirdly personal space I've been pulled.

Them, Onah says again.

I want to ask who they are, but I stop the words before they make it to my tongue. Jørans don't name things like we do. He's already told me who they are.

The musty, metallic scent/taste of *Them* lingers on my tongue, coating my throat.

Humans weren't the first species to attempt colonising Jørn, every school kid knows that. We were merely the first to survive the experience.

There were others before us, a race who built their homes under the ground and who, like those first humans, were unable to survive the Pollen, the spore that saturates the planet's atmosphere. Like us they were blind to the Jørans presence, seeing only animals where something much fiercer and more complicated stood. Unlike us though, the Jørans drove them out.

Those were the memories I'd experienced. *Them* were the aliens who'd found Jørn almost a thousand years before humans.

They were the beings Onah thought were eating our ship.

Except I hadn't seen any big, pale bipeds demolishing the bulkheads. Just fug.

Okay. That doesn't make sense. I mean, even less sense than usual, and I mean, usually things kinda happen and you run with it, but you know there's some kind of logic behind it. This is just screwy.

And now that I think about it…

Something's been bugging me about Onah, something more than the too-personal sensation. It feels… full, like it's ship soccer night and I'm standing in the middle of the Atrium with the rest of the crew. All of us crowded around the pitch, except instead of watching the game, everyone is staring at *me*.

I rub the back of my neck, my hand brushing Dude, cuddled up under my ear, making himself as small as possible. Which, FYI, is *really* quiet. I'd totally forgotten he was with me. I wonder how he'd done it, how Onah hadn't sensed him, how an eter could have two people and yet be full.

And I wonder why it's so dark. What's Onah's eter like that he's got to hide it?

The light switches on in my head, realisation lighting up the area around me like a floodlight. The darkness pushes back.

I was wrong. This is not Onah's eter.

I spin around, trying to pierce the dark, focusing on the dense shadows. It's not like focusing on the mist, or the lightning. The shadows resist. Sticky and stubborn, trying to wriggle out of my sight, and that's when I know, *really* know. And once that happens... I may not be a telepath or a Regan, able to read minds and create a collective big enough to take on the water-kin but I'm strong. And I'm an empath.

The *emote* rips through the eter, a tsunami of joy and light shredding the darkness to pieces.

Surprise. Shock. Panic.

Jørans don't have empaths. It's a human talent, and one they haven't quite figured out, let alone know how to counter. The kin hadn't stood a chance.

Other emotions follow in the wake of the *emote*, rising from the spots where the shadows once stood. Now all I see are rucnarts and qwans, throwing their heads and shaking their wings, the ground around them rich with the orange of surprise.

The only one who doesn't seem surprised is Onah, but I guess that's because he's too busy trying to keep fear from saturating the space around him. I guess it's hard, what with the snaking veins of yellow winding up his legs and around his torso, binding his wings to his chest. I'd be scared too. In fact, I don't need to glance down to see the puke-yellow of fear snaking up my ankles.

Fug was one thing. Ancient alien enemies were another. But being surrounded by a double handful of scared, angry Jørans was something else entirely. Onah might not eat me, but none of the others are that friendly. H'Rawd in particular seems hungry.

The rucnart shakes off the surprise of being revealed first. One second the tree-kin leader is on the other side of the eter, the next he's snarling, shoving his hot, stinky breath in my face.

Maybe hitting them with the *emote* hadn't been a good idea.

Anger and frustration roll of him in waves, turning the air a murky red that hugs my skin and tries to dig thorns into my flesh. Sharp, angry pulses beat again my shields, the kind of rhythmic pulse I recognise as words but can't make out 'cause I'm not a telepath and all, and h'Rawd has forgotten to mould his thoughts into something I can understand.

'I can't understand what you're saying.'

H'Rawd snarls, shoving teeth and a barrage of images in my face.

I stagger. They're flying by too fast to make out, but one catches my attention. It's the tang of blood, the hot taste of it in my mouth. I see a man who looks like Dad but isn't, with dark hair and tilted eyes, green instead of the dark brown of my father's. He runs, leaving a trail of fear, as electric as blood. I catch the memory, hold it tight. Others whip past; some cling to it, bringing with them other images, more emotions. Frustration. Fear. Defeat. Anger. A pulsing disc. Human faces. Fascination. Excitement. Argument. Discord. The captain saying 'No'. Dad holding the other man back, hands on the other man's shoulders, while I lash my tail and bare my fangs.

Fear rides the air, coming from different places, with different meanings, but all of it tastes the same.

I stagger, and rip myself away from the flood, and then it's Onah's turn.

He pushes h'Rawd aside, or rather, pushes me back. There's no movement though, no hands on my shoulders. One moment h'Rawd has his muzzle in my face and the next he's a distant spot, hidden behind Onah's bulk.

You will do as we need.

Unlike h'Rawd, Onah's voice is perfectly modulated, his thoughts sinking into my skin with none of the sharp edges or spikes of the rucnart's. None of the anger either, although there's still that rough edge of fear snaking up his wings.

'I don't get it. What do you need? Why me?'

You are awake.

'But—'

You are awake, and you have the ability. "Ability" is said with a hint of awe and frustration and a brief reminder of the *emote* that shredded the kins' darkness like Old Terran paper.

'But—' I figure if I keep saying "but" Onah might actually tell me something useful, like what the fuck it is they *need* me to do.

You must, or we die.

'That's not helpful. *What* do you need me to do?'

The push comes out of nowhere. It's not the same push that Onah used to get me away from h'Rawd, not a physical relocation. It's a mental push. The kind that only telepaths, and really powerful ones at that, can accomplish.

It hits me in the back of the head. There's no colour to it, no emotion. I can't even tell if there's any *thought*. It's a ball of nothing, blasting through my shields like they're not even there, sinking into my psyche with razors tipped in ice. It doesn't hurt, not yet at least. And then it's gone. The razors, the push, the Jørans. Only Onah is left. I know, because the eter feels less full and more personal, like my face is smooshed up against the qwan's neck and all I can breathe is the dusty, coppery scent of his feathers.

I have a moment to blink, to wonder what in the Old Terra just happened, before the pain hits.

Qwans aren't exactly the gentlest of psions. Onah's better than most. He at least sees us hybrids as something a little higher on the evolutionary chain than dirt. They were like that before the war, or at least, that's what Mac's dad says, and a hundred years in space hasn't changed them much. A bit like the AI and her struggle with physics-defying psionics.

Still, it was Onah who lead that push. It's like I've been stabbed in the brain. My eyes are blurring, and dark, inky swirls of pain are winding up my legs. If I can figure out how to use my vocal cords, I'd scream, but I'm too busy trying to figure out how to keep *being*.

Seconds turn to hours. Fire is eating me up from the inside out, tendrils of it shooting out my nose, leaking from my ears, turning my hair to inky flame. I feel like my skin should melt, slough off my bones, leaving red pulsing muscle behind.

It doesn't happen. Instead the pain vanishes, leaving nothing behind, not even the slicing, sliding sense of the kins' claws digging through my skull.

There's a command sphere in my head. I can't sense it, but I *know* it's there, like I know I have five digits on each hand and my hair is black. Know it like I know I'm a boy, even if I was born otherwise.

I stand.

Onah's studying me, all four eyes open, his beak raised, both sets of wings tight to his sides, impassive but for the green threads of anxiety joining the yellow swirls of fear around his talons.

'Why?' We both know what I'm asking, even if I don't yell it in his face. Even if I *want* to yell it in his face. Even if I want to swear and rage and hit him with all of the fear and hurt filling my chest. I may not be able to open a stasis pod or pry open an emergency hatch, but I'm good at some things. You can't have focus without control. And no one out-focuses me. Plus, yelling in a qwan's face usually gets your nose bitten off.

We need you.

There's desperation in his words, the emotion mixed up with snatches of memory, flashes that are gone almost as soon as they appear, but I catch a few. They hit me in the head, made sticky by Onah's emotions. I close my eyes, trying to keep my feet. There's the shiny, oval thing, pulsing and squeezing like a metallic heart. With this image comes more emotion, a hint of fear, a spike of desperation, a frantic, scared sensation like I'm running out of time. Chasing it all, comes something else, something that's… wrong. Slippery, like a mirage or a ghost. A pressure against my psyche that isn't and is, a shadow seen in the dark out the corner of my eye, that disappears when I focus on it.

It's almost enough to dissolve the anger building in my chest, and for a moment the emotion slips, replaced by the fear and frantic need permeating Onah's memories. Almost. Right up until the moment I sense him *pushing*. The memories didn't slip past Onah's shields. Qwans are some of the best psions Jørn has to offer. They can control the twitch of an insect's wings while still directing the swarm. And Onah is old, canny, and he knows me. Taught me.

My muscles are shaking. Fine little quivers that run up and down my arms, making my skin twitch. In my chest, fear is turning to hate, twisting in on itself as the hurt, the betrayal fades. None of it stains the eter though.

Control is everything in an eter, even when it's not yours.

'You could have asked.'

Onah tilts his head, swinging his beak to the side and studying me with the eyes on the right side of his face. The red upper eye catches me, reaching out and grabbing me by the shoulders, trying to pin me in place.

I shrug him off.

We will ask next time.

'I'm not coming here again.'

Yes, you will. And then he pushes me out.

CHAPTER ELEVEN

Cold greets me. A bone-deep, icicle-breeding cold that bites my nose and makes my sides shudder. Dude's still tucked up under my chin; a tiny ball of warmth reminding me that being warm is a thing.

Getting up is hard. Uncurling from my nest of plasform and junk, surrendering the little heat it provides, seems like a really bad idea but a little voice at the back of head, the one that reminds me of Dad, is telling me otherwise. Plus, Dude feels sick again, that too-full sensation of his weighing down my stomach.

Moving generates a thread of heat, enough to get me to my feet, but not enough to stop the shudders rippling up my sides.

As awesome as shipsuits are, there're not nanoskins. They don't regulate my temperature because *Citlali* does that... or is supposed to.

I'm pretty sure it's colder here than it was on Stasis. My fingertips are blue and I've lost the feeling in my lips.

The enviros are fucked, that's the only reason for the cold. At least there's still oxygen, even if breathing it is like sucking down ice.

So, new goal. Don't stop moving.

Besides, sitting here on my arse isn't going to fix Dude.

I need to get to Medical but he doesn't have that much time, not unless I can find a clear run through Lab One to Central, and from the jungle of fug we burnt through getting *here*, that's not going to happen.

So. Medical is out. At least for now. That doesn't leave a lot of options, but at least I'm on Lab Two. That's something. Something that may save Dude's fuzzy butt.

Citlali's not any old ship. It's one of five ships sent out from Jørn on a mission to explore the galaxy, and like any good expedition, it's packed with scientists. Lots and lots of scientists, the kind who like sticking their noses in alien crap and seeing what they can do with it. Which isn't good for the alien crap but is great for me. And Dude. I just have to find Mae Liu's lab.

There's no sign of the fug on this deck, and that's about as good as it gets in an attempt to find Mae Liu's lab.

It shouldn't be this hard. I know Lab Two like I know my bedroom. Dad's lab is on this deck, and I spend enough time wandering the corridors that I can find my way around blindfolded with the gravity turned off. Literally.

But... I don't know. Either Mae Liu got another lab assignment before the last stasis cycle, or the Lab AI is messing with me. Seriously messing with me.

Given the fact that Lab doesn't have a sense of humour, that seems unlikely.

Unfortunately, it doesn't change the fact that Mae Liu's lab isn't where it's supposed to be.

'Lab!' My voice echoes in the corridor.

As on Stasis, Mae Liu's should be on the third of the middle rings, although this time, it's not because she's more important than anyone else, but because she doesn't need access to the docking bay, which suits her. Mae Liu hates going EVA, and she doesn't so much study alien stuff as figure out how to apply what the others have discovered, to the ship. And us.

The curve on the third mid-ring distorts sound, and my voice echoes back at me in a dozen fractured words, all yelling the same thing.

I wait for the echoes to fade and try again. Just for luck.

'Lab!'

Was that a ripple on the wall, or a trick of my imagination?

I move away from the hatch and press my hand to the wall. 'Lab? Hey, you there?'

Nothin— Wait, what was that? Further down the corridor another ripple of light catches my eye, there then gone, like a mirage. What the fuck?

'Did you see that?' I ask Dude.

Dude *fuzzes*, the sound slow, weighed down by the too-full feeling and the beginnings of fiery blades running down his spine.

I scratch his head. 'We're getting there.'

I follow the ripple.

It leads me to the outer ring and around the other side of the ship, jumping first from one side of the corridor to the other and back again, like some kind of demented lightning bug. Rippling once and then gone.

Maybe Lab's vocals are on the fritz and this is the only way she can communicate. But then, what was with the flashes of light on the walls? Why not use words or appear herself? Was there something wrong with the holo-emitters?

I tell myself to give up worrying about it, but that leaves room for other worries to intrude. Ones less pleasant, accompanied by the sweet smell of rotting flesh and the iron tang of blood.

Worry about the holos. It won't give you nightmares.

Thankfully, the ripples stop before thinking about what's making Lab coy leads my thoughts right back to where they were.

Lab's given up on ripples, throwing them over in favour of a giant pulsing beacon that I'm pretty sure is bright enough to burn out the emitters, right after they burn out my retinas.

All throwing my hands up and shutting my eyes does is turn the sun-like glare into an angry red glow.

'Lab, I see it! Tone it down.'

The blaze vanishes.

It takes a little bit for my eyes to figure that out.

I lower my arms and blink.

The world's a little blurry but I'm pretty sure I'm standing in front of a door.

Another blink.

I'm going to have stars in my eyes for the next year, but there's definition in the haze of colour now, and yeah, that's a door.

One final blink and the door comes fully into focus, an all-too-familiar off-white hatch with a long deep scratch at shin height, running through the door and down the corridor.

This is Dad's lab, but the name over the door isn't his.

AD Tudor floats high enough I can't miss it.

I know I'm in the right place. I *know* I am. For one, there's that scratch in the holowall, a deep scar of pale grey, a metre and seventy-seven centimetres long. I know that because Captain—

A clawed hand reaching out of biogel...

I shake the image away.

It doesn't matter how I know how long the scar is, it matters that it marks where I crashed Dad's hoversled and that it was right in front of his lab.

The second way I know that shit is weird is this; I don't know who AD Tudor is. Not a clue or inkling or anything else that might be an idea. That might not be a problem if I didn't live on a ship. But I do. I know everyone. Every. One.

Whoever the fuck AD Tudor is, they don't live on *Citlali*.

The lab door is open. A crack between the frame and the thin plasteel shell. My body doesn't seem to care that its brain is still trying to figure out what the fuck is going on. It's shifting muscles and squeezing tendons, lifting bones and curling appendages and before I know it, I'm opening the door that says AD Tudor and entering Dad's lab.

Dad's *not* AD Tudor. He's Jori Darzi, a tall, dark-haired man who smiles as he drags me out of bed and frowns like it hurts when he grounds me, but even though the name on the door is wrong, the insides are all his, right down to the acid burn on the decking and the black mark in the centre bench.

My legs take me inside, my feet steer me past the bench with its acid burn, down the aisle between it and the shelves full of rocks and jars of minerals, all the way down the back, into the little cubby that houses the food dispenser and the toilet. They stop at the back bulkhead, the only bare and empty space in the lab. In *any* lab.

In all the hours I've spent in here, watching Dad do his thing, that blank space has never struck me as strange, but now... Now, with my feet holding me rooted in place and my hand lifting, I'm thinking that it's more than strange. It's downright suspicious. Or maybe that's the command sphere blooming again deep in my skull. I can't feel it, but just because I can't sense something doesn't mean it's not there. Plus, there's the disconnect between body and brain and the way my fingers know to press that spot right *there.*

The bulkhead parts, splits right down the middle and sucks itself into the wall on either side, revealing a small slither of space beyond, just big enough to wedge a person.

I wish it was a body behind the wall. This is worse.

It's hard to imagine worse than a corpse. A minute ago I would have said a rotting corpse, but this... I really wish it was a dead person.

The black oval stuck in the wall is bigger than my chest and pulses like a metallic heart. Finger-width strands move under the surface like muscles, contracting and expanding in slow motion, and there's this impression coming off of it, like being in the ice hull except... creepier.

I know what this is. The knowledge flows up from the back of my head, a strange mix of memories that are mine and yet aren't.

It's the disc I saw in h'Rawd's and Onah's memories. The thing AD and Dad fought over. And with that realisation come other memories, filling in the blank places in my head like they'd always been there, waiting for me to remember. And I know now what the argument was about, can remember the human words thudding in my ears, loud and jarring, making my fur bristle and skin clench even after all these years. I watch blood flush human skin, smell the anger in the air, strong enough to match mine, and I remember wishing that these hairless beasts had teeth and claws, could hear the song of the beacon so that they would *understand*.

The thing in the bulkhead isn't Jøran and I know, right down to the pit of my stomach, that it's bad. There's a sense about it, a sinister, half-felt tingle up my spine, like a shadow lurking in the corner of my eye. I've felt it before, not only in the Jørans' memories but here, on the *Citlali*, except it's stronger here. I can taste it, like old meat, musty and sharp, like it's got teeth.

The disc repulses me and yet…

My arm has a life of its own, muscles tensing, fingers stretching. The oval seems to pause a moment and then start up again, beating harder and faster than before as my fingers inch closer.

'The specimen was recovered in the Megora system.' The AI's voice booms out of the walls and I swear, if we were in orbit, I'd have left it.

An AI floats next to me, or part of one. My heart settles back in my chest as I recognise the small green head and bland expression. Looks like Lab found a working holo emitter somewhere.

'I don't remember Megora.'

'It is the first system out from Jørn. You were not yet conceived.'

Right. Well, that would explain that.

'What is it?' I point to the oval.

'I do not know.'

'But… it's here.'

Lab stares at me.

'How can you not know what it is?'

'Details regarding the object are sealed.'

'But you know it came from Megora.'

Lab blinks, and suddenly it's like there's something floating in the air between us, some secret meaning. It's probably h'Rawd's memories still taking up space my head, mixing with the creepiness pulsing off the disc, making me see things or rather, feel things, that aren't there but… but Lab *never* blinks. Never.

I step back, pressing into the bulkhead behind, wishing I could melt right through as I remember the mad expression in Ag's eyes, and the malice that had hung in the air.

Deep breaths, Kuma, deep breaths. It's probably a glitch.

The AI blinks again. There's a pause and then she does it again, eyelids moving in a rapid flutter before she stops.

My heart's beating hard. Thumping against my ribs, and I'm halfway up the bulkhead at my back, deciding whether or not skidding over the top of the lab benches will get me out of here faster than a simple mad dash to the door.

Lab is still staring at me, expression as bland as the bulkhead, like she's waiting for something.

I stare back, trying not to breathe too loud, in case the sound sets her off.

Lab floats closer. 'The records are sealed, Kuma Darzi.'

What? 'The records?'

Lab's head turns transparent, or more transparent, a barely-there ghost over the shiny, pulsing oval stuck in the bulkhead. 'Only the captain is authorised to unseal them.'

I swallow back memories. 'The captain's dead.'

'Authority has passed to the XO.'

The memories are crawling up the back of my throat. I swallow harder. 'Dead too.'

'The Chief Medical Officer.'

I shake my head. 'No.'

Lab's expression doesn't change, but there's something in her eyes, or maybe it's that she's moved closer, her nose almost touching mine, and there's nowhere to look but into those all-green orbs. 'All authority rests with the highest ranking, functioning crew member.'

'But I'm the only one…' Oh.

Right.

'Lab, unseal the…' I wave at the oval. 'The object's record.'

Of all the things I expected to unfold in the space before me, it wasn't the captain. She's looking out at me, light hair and pale skin, her eyes the same brilliant blue I remembered, but instead of anger making them hard, they're filled with something else, an emotion that makes them big and liquid. Fear. The captain was afraid.

'Play it.'

'If you're seeing this, things have gone horribly wrong. The beacon we found in Megora must be destroyed. Do it now. We should have jettisoned it when Onah asked us, but AD's argument was compelling, and I could not bring myself to let such an important piece of Jørn's history go. But I fear that AD has done more than study it, and now that he's missing…' Her mouth thins, and lines appear in her forehead. Pain? Worry? More than fear, more than uncertainty. The expression makes my stomach curl in on itself and my heart contract in sympathy. 'I don't think we'll find the body.'

She shakes her head and her expression firms, becomes the stern face I'm used to seeing, before she continues.

'Onah is reporting a new wavelength in the Aer, something neither he nor the other Jørans can pin down.' She pauses. 'It's the beacon. I'm sure AD found a way to amplify its signal, and then hid it. He may have even tampered with the *Citlali's* navigation, but I can find no trace of it.

'The qwans always seem so in control, but when Onah came to see me he was scared, shaken in a way I haven't seen since the war. Whomever that beacon is calling, they terrify the Jørans more than Regan's final stand.' She leans close. 'I don't want to meet the beings who can do that. Not yet, not ever. Find the beacon and destroy it, before it's too late.'

The captain disappears.

I'm left staring at the shiny, pulsating oval in the bulkhead. At the beacon.

I guess I found it. Except I hadn't, not really.

Lab pops into being, her green head obscuring the beacon.

I'd been led here.

'You knew where it was all along.'

Lab doesn't respond, just blinks at me.

I peel myself from the bulkhead. I'm pretty sure I'm getting this now. Lab wants to tell me something, but for some reason she can't come right out and say it. I have to ask.

'Why didn't you tell the captain where AD hid the beacon?'

Lab blinks.

It's like playing twenty questions, but instead of a yes or no, I'm getting eyelids.

'Lab, unseal *all* records concerning the beacon.'

'I cannot.'

'Why?'

'You are not authorised.'

'I'm the highest ranking, functional crew member.'

Lab doesn't respond.

'Who is authorised?'

'Jori Darzi and Arthur David Tudor.'

Ooo-kay. Well, that puts a stop to that.

We stare at each other for a long moment.

Dude fuzzes against my neck.

'You require a path the Medical.'

'Yes.'

Lab nods, a strange motion for a bodiless head, and then a map springs up before me. 'You will need tools,' she says.

CHAPTER TWELVE

There's more than one way to skin a cat. Dad likes to say that, I'm not really sure why, or why you'd want to skin a cat. It seems kinda stupid, and messy, and painful for the cat, but maybe Old Terra felines didn't feel things like that? I don't know. There's a lot I don't know and I'm getting tired of that, of bouncing around this ship not knowing what I'm doing or where I'm going or if anything I'm doing is worth anything.

I'm tired. Tired and cold and alone. Tired of holding on to memories and not letting the shit at the back of my brain in. Tired. Tired. Tired.

Maybe, if this doesn't work, I'll go crawl into my pod and sleep through the rest of this. Whatever this is.

It's the fullness in Dude's belly that's driving me now, giving me the energy to rip the cover off the air duct.

After dumping the whole beacon thing on me, Lab had pulled a blueprint of *Citlali* from her databanks. It'd been full of blank spots, like something had eaten it, but the bits we needed were still there. Mostly.

It was the fuzzy, half-eaten bit that's worrying me.

I peer down the shaft. There's not much to see. The shaft is a pit. No lights, only blackness. Deep, dark, endless and at the end of it… That bit's fuzzy, fuzzy like the fug-eaten star on the speedway hatch. If I'm lucky, at the end of it is Medical. If I'm not… Well, that's what the drone's for.

I heft the head-sized sphere scrounged from Dad's lab. Drones don't need lights. It doesn't take much to sync it with my palm unit. A few swipes across its control panel, a little bit of spit to connect it to the biocomp and voila. I'm wired for sound, video and a few senses usually reserved for Old Terran superheroes, like heat and x-ray vision.

I drop the drone down the shoot.

It plummets.

I just about plummet in after it.

Shit. Was it supposed to do that?

Did I turn it on?

I open my palm, scrambling for the controls.

Telemetry spreads over my hand, visuals and heat and electromagnetic readouts. And there. Anti-gravs.

I hit the button.

There's no crash, no shattering plasform and biogel echoing up from the bottom of the shaft.

My heart slows. The vid above my palm is black, but the telemetry is still flowing, filling the other screens with data I'm not really sure how to read. I mean, I know *how* to read it, heat is heat after all, either hot or cold, and speed is... well, you get the idea. I don't know what it's telling me about the shaft. But hey, at least the drone isn't scrap.

I activate the vid.

A glow rises from deep in the shaft, and on my palm unit I see...

'Crap.'

Fug. Lots and lots of fug.

And now I know why the drone didn't die.

The fug's all over the shoot, thick enough that it's caught the drone.

A hit of the thrusters and the drone pops free. No warning lights yet. The fug hasn't had a chance to eat the plasform.

I guide the drone upwards. It doesn't get better. I'm not sure how long the shaft is, but about thirty metres down the fug starts. Which means there's a fuck-load of distance between it and Med.

Shit.

I wasn't getting down the shaft without help. Lots of help.

Like the fire and brimstone kind.

The shaft was too narrow to fit me and the Franken, but... I eye the flamethrower.

★

In the end, I don't bother with finesse or stripping the power out, I point the barrel down the tube, tape the trigger on and let go.

Probably not my brightest move, but the engineering shit was giving me a headache.

The explosion rings in my ears.

I guess that was the end of the Franken.

I rub my ears clear of the sound and peer down the shaft. A red glow is rising from the blackness, gentle heat against my face and the scent of soot. It's fading fast, but the smell of carbon on the warm updraft is encouraging. I send the drone down again, holding my breath and letting it out again in a rush when it hovers at the bottom of the shaft. One-hundred and fifty metres of air-duct and not a trace of fug. Unless you counted the ash.

I'm not.

Leaving the drone where it is, I check the grav harness wrapped around my waist. It's a thick white band of plasform and biogel, two bulbous ends on the points of my hips and another over my butt. They glow solid white, signalling full batteries. A separate indicator flashes on the screen over my palm, along with a little warning light telling me the stabiliser is damaged. I'm ignoring it.

There wasn't a lot of choice of supplies in Dad's lab and the stabiliser wasn't that important anyway, not when all I need is a few minutes of antigravity.

I pick up Dude, tuck him into the little pocket I'd made over my chest and swing my legs over the side of the shaft. A deep breath, set the delay on the harness's grav activation to two seconds, and push off the edge.

Those initial two seconds suck.

The antigrav kicking in sucks harder.

One moment the belt is glowing, the next it's blazing with light and I'm trying to keep hold of my stomach as the belt tried to push what little is left in it, out.

As I'm winding the bile back down my throat, that stabiliser I wasn't going to worry about? I should have worried about it.

Not my brightest idea.

The grav harness is flashing a frenetic dance of red and the readout above my palm is doing the same, only it's also showing how long the shaft is and how far I have to fall.

Really not a good idea.

My breath is stuck somewhere between my lungs and my throat, and my heart is beating out a rapid tattoo in time with the warning lights. There's a thought caught somewhere between my lungs and heart, that if I don't move, the harness will last longer; that somehow me not moving will make my mass less, take the strain off the power reserves.

Another part of my brain, the bit that sounds like Grea, tells me I'm an idiot and if I pass out from lack of air, I'll really be in the shit. It's got a point, but I'm still holding my breath.

There's no lights in the shaft, only the mad red blink of the harness and the equally mad glow of my palm unit. I can't see the bottom, can only make out the smooth sides and the darker lines where the steelcrete plates fit together. If it weren't for those lines, I could fool myself into believing I was hanging there, not moving, going neither up nor down. At first the lines move past at a leisurely pace, three breaths between joins, and then two, and then one and now faster. Two lines to a breath, three. Or they would, if I was still breathing instead of imagining myself smooshed against the steelcrete, a Kuma pancake with a dollop of Dude on top.

The harness blinks faster and now there's a warning flashing over my palm, and the shadow lines are ripping past and I really wish I'd taken the other harness as my palm unit keeps searching for the

bottom—

The harness squeals. Dies.

The light dies with it.

I fall.

I can't see anything.

Am I actually falling?

Pain lances up my legs. Meets my side, my face.

There are stars. Not the pinpricks of suns, but bright supernovas, exploding along with the pain in my head. Then, nothing.

Dude is sitting on my face.

How long have I been out? With the harness dead, there's no light. I press the spot by my elbow, groaning as the movement makes my head throb and pain ricochet through my back.

Open my palm and my biocomp flares to life.

The light has new pain stabbing at my eyes. I squeeze them shut and try to ignore the throb in my skull. I want to lay here, safe and sound on at the bottom of the shaft, away from fug and death.

There's a soft patter down my chest and then a *skritch skritch* coming from my waist.

I ignore it. Everything hurts and I'm tired, so tired.

SKRITCH.

I open my eyes.

Another soft patter, this time up my chest and there's Dude, wicked little claws extended and raised above my face.

'Holy Terra!'

Adrenalin shoots through my system, chasing the tiredness away and obliterating the headache. I'm on my feet—

BANG

Ow.

My knees hit the deck, one hand reaching out to brace myself while the other rubs the back of my head. The painkilling effect of adrenalin flees before the burst of light in front of my eyes when my head hit the top of the duct.

I peer upwards.

The movement sends new spikes of pain through my skull, so I lift my sight enough to see the edge of the duct I'd brained myself on.

Dude climbs onto the back of my hand, a ball of warmth and fluff, a *fuzz*. It's thready, and there are hints of pain in it, staining the golden presence black. It's enough to remind me of my mission.

I tuck him in the pouch on my chest and only wince a little as my back sends up a flare of abused muscles, while something in my side adds a fiery spike of protest.

'Okay, Dude. Let's get you to Medical.'

I press the spot on my elbow and my palm-unit springs to life. There's enough light from the screen to spot the drone; still in one piece but dark and rolled up against the side of the duct. A swipe across my screen and for a couple of heartbeats, nothing happens and I wonder if I crushed the drone when I fell, but then it flickers, a rapid pulse that makes my head pound harder, before it solidifies.

Another couple of swipes, and even if I don't have a map, at least I can see where I'm going. There are only two directions available, so I pick one and start crawling. It seems to take forever; every shuffle forward sends pain through my nerves. My ribs are on fire, and it feels like there's jagged bits of plasglas in my knees, grinding against bone. Then there's the fire running up and down my back. The worst is my head, the way my skull seems too small for my brain. It's making it hard to think, hard to move and there are moments when I realise I can't remember what I was thinking the second before, can't remember how I got *here*.

Between two of those moments, I pass through a sharp blue glow that's strung up across the tunnel. It seems familiar, tickling a memory of another blue light, one that sparked around a big round door protecting something…

The memory escapes me, and trying to pull it out is making it harder to put one hand in front of the other so I push it aside.

There's a tingle as I pass through the light. The air on the other side smells different, cleaner, without the heavy scent of carbon and soot.

I stop then, just for a bit, to give my eyes a rest and chase away the pounding in my skull.

It's Dude's *fuzzing* that wakes me, reminds me that I have a job to do. I follow the glow of the drone, and when I remember, I hope against hope that I picked the right direction.

The top of my head smacks into the drone, and the next thing I know I'm tumbling through a hole in the floor, catching myself on the edge long enough to halt my descent a second. And then I'm tumbling through nothing and...

I'm standing. Wobbling down a corridor and I'm not quite sure how that happened but I'm not complaining. My feet seem to know where they're going, or maybe that's the glow of the drone leading me on.

My knees don't hurt anymore. In fact, nothing really hurts. Not my ribs, not my back, not anything. Not even my head. I can't feel anything, and something deep in my brain suggests that that's probably bad, but the rest of me is too tired to do anything about it, so I log the thought and keep following the drone.

I little bit of me wonders where the fug is, and then my legs stop.

The drone is floating on ahead, and I try to move after it, but even though I can lift my feet, there's something in the way of my thighs.

I look down.

It's a wide, flat thing, as high as my waist and the length of my body.

Huh.

I know what that is. I do. The name's not coming though.

There's a blank bit there, a little reset, and now I'm around the wide flat thing, trying to find the thing I was following...

The room I'm in is dark, and there are more of those flat things laid out in a circle around a clear space, and in the clear space there's a glowy thing floating above another glowy thing stuck in the floor and...

Oh yeah. The drone. I'm following the drone.

I shuffle forward.

The drone's right there, except it's not moving this time, and that's not really a bad thing because all this walking is making me tired and...

...And...

Huh, that glowy floor thing sure is pretty.

I wonder what happens if I touch it. I've got to make my knees work first. I'm pretty sure they bend...

Turns out I don't need to make my knees work. One of my forward shuffles brings my foot close enough to smudge the light and the next thing I know, there's even more light pouring out the floor and a face, lilac with dark eyes, staring at me. The mouth is moving, but I'm not really hearing what's coming out of it because a thought's just dawned.

Slowly, because it's taking longer than it should to get my hands moving, I scoop Dude out of the pouch on my chest and hold him up.

'Fix him.'

CHAPTER THIRTEEN

I'm not really sure what happened after I told Med to fix Dude, but I woke on a med bed, remembering flashing lights and belly flopping on the nearest flat surface. It must have been a med bed because that was where I woke, staring at the shadows on the ceiling, a spike trying to drive itself through my head and my mouth tasting like someone had shat in it.

It's not a good way to wake up, but I guess it wasn't as bad as being eaten by fug.

There'd been a little drone, not quite as big as my fist, hovering by the side of the bed, and when I tried to sit up, it flashed and beeped loud enough to sending me crashing back into darkness.

Waking the second time, my head didn't pound anymore, the old-shit taste in the back of my throat was gone and instead of the ceiling I was treated to a closeup of the drone.

'Hey,' I said. Or tried. My voice had come out as a croak worthy of an oad-hawk, sounding more like I was hacking up phlegm instead of words. Still, the drone seemed to speak croakeese.

It bobbed and floated to the side, shining a little cone of light on the hover tray beside the med.

Water.

Oh man, I'd never been so glad to see water.

I was sitting, legs swinging off the bed, gulping the water down like I'd never seen the stuff, then I noticed the small army of med drones hovering around the bed.

A lump the size of a moon had formed in my chest at about the same time the med bots pounced.

That'd been hours and lots of prodding and poking ago.

I didn't so much escape the bots, more they let me go. Turns out, falling down an air shaft hadn't been good for me and there'd been only so much they could do while I was unconscious and the only living thing with opposable digits who was out of stasis on the whole ship.

I'm still on the med bed, but instead of being flat on my back or surrounded by a swarm of bots, I'm sitting cross-legged, or as close as I can get with the bulky pads around my knees and a brace holding my left shoulder in place.

Broken cartilage and a dislocated shoulder had been the least of my troubles, because somewhere along the line, a couple of bots injected me with tubes full of nano-meds, and not the fun blue ones either. Nope, they stuck me with the pink stuff, the kind that spread under your skin and went to work on your insides, patching up holes and repairing bone with flamethrowers.

I guess they've fixed all the really important stuff and are working on my shoulder now, cause it doesn't hurt quite so much as I reach for the water glass beside the bed.

The one time I'd made it off the bed, hobbling my way over to the med unit in the corner, trying to peer through the plasglas, searching for Dude, I'd quickly been herded back. You wouldn't reckon tiny med bots could make you do anything, but you haven't seen them en masse, flashing and buzzing around your head, waving hypo-sticks in your face like they know how to use them.

They'd let me park myself on the bed closest to the med unit, and there I'd stayed. Less because of the threat of death by med bot and more because my knees hurt, although not as much as they had before, and I silently thank the nano-meds.

Beyond her initial appearance as a floating lilac head, Med hadn't stopped in to say hi, or check up or anything. I guess that's what she had the bots for, and you know, doctors and stuff, but still, it was a little disconcerting. And lonely.

The glow from the med unit sheds enough light to see the shadows and not much else, but I found a glow and it's enough to work by. Not that there's much to work. The Franken is dead, a charred mess of biogel and plasform somewhere back in the air ducts I used to get here.

At least the enviros are still working here, and the bots have a seemingly endless supply of ration bars.

It's been hours since I checked on Dude. Hours to ponder and worry and try to figure out how I'm going to get back to Ag. If I even want to go back to Ag. The memory of Ag standing there with that mad glint in her eye shivers through my skull. There's no other way to Hatchery though. Maybe if I'm really fast, I can blitz through Ag deck and shove the new critter sequence into Hatchery.

It's all moot though, if I can't get through the fug. I need another Franken-thrower, or a blaster or an army of drones. But then, if I had drones, I wouldn't need to take the new gene sequence to Ag, I could load it up and—

Something moves in the gloom and I'm on my feet before the alarm finishes skittering up my spine. The pounding of my heart is the only sound in the lab. It's the tension, I swear it's the tension. It's holding my spine still, fuelling the rapid beat of my pulse and—

There it is again, a darker shadow at the corner of my eye, skittering along the floor.

I'm around the workbench, torch in hand, before I have time to wonder what I'm doing and what I'm actually chasing. There's an image of a grey-green ball of tendrils floating in my mind's eye, eating the med beds and leaving a sticky trail of fug in its wake.

More movement and I'm on my knees, wincing in pain as they hit the deck and thinking perhaps this is not the best position to be in, not with the Franken in charred pieces and my face way too close to—

A fist-sized blot of darkness detaches itself from the nearest shadow and leaps at my face.

There's half a second in which to scream.

I should have kept my mouth shut, maybe then I wouldn't have ended up with a mouth full of fluff and a couple of paws.

At least it's not fug.

I spit the critter out.

It plops on the ground and chitters at me.

The critter's smaller and darker than Dude, with a short dull pelt that's ragged around the edges, like it's been eaten.

I reach for it— And snap my hand back.

That's not a critter.

'Onah.' My voice echoes, bouncing off the med beds and benches, and all of a sudden, I feel alone.

Kuma. His voice rings in my mind, and I'm not staring at the critter any more but the massive qwan on the inside of my eyelids. *Follow me.*

'No.'

Come.

I sit back and cross my arms. Pains shoots through my relocated shoulder, but it's no longer enough to do more than momentarily disturb my frown (thank you nano-meds).

Behind my eyes, Onah cocks his head, considering me with his lower eyes, the critter at my knees mirroring him. Several long moments pass, stretching out into infinity as we stare each other down.

I'm starting to feel weird, nervous and uncertain, and a worm of doubt is wriggling its way past my resolve. Then Onah blinks and it's gone.

He dips his head, both eyes closing. *Please, youngling.*

I've never heard a qwan say please before. Never heard them ask for anything. They usually make requests like they're stating facts, as if reality will warp around them simply because they said so.

That's the only reason I'm on my feet, following the Onah/critter out of the lab. We don't go far, not out into the fug jungle.

Onah/critter leads me to a corner and bounds up the bulkhead like it's got glue on its paws. Up, up, up, to a dark square hole in the ceiling, more than big enough for a critter to slip through and maybe big enough for me too, with a little bit of contortion.

I stare up at it. 'You want me to follow in there?'

Onah/critter sticks its head out of the hole. *Yes.*

Well. Okay. It's not the squeezing through that's a problem, it's the getting *up* there with still-not-quite healed knees and probably the getting out, and maybe, probably, the fug crawling all over the ship.

One problem at a time Kuma. One. Problem. At. A. Time.

With each thought I'm looking around the med bay, clocking the chairs and the table, weighing it all in my mind as I consider the flamethrowers still working inside my legs and... Yeah, that'll do.

I'm sweating by the time I climb my mountain of furniture, and maybe that helps a little as I wriggle my way into the air duct. I figure that's what it is, although it could as easily be a critter highway, except that'd be smaller, 'cause critters are, you know, small.

I push the torch ahead of me, grateful for the duct's smooth surface as I pull myself along with one elbow and a whole lot of wriggling in a lopsided shuffle-slide. There's enough room for my shoulders and I've already brained myself on the top; my knees aren't having much fun either, and I'm pretty sure I'll have bots are chasing me with more tubes of pink nano-meds when I get back to Medical. If I get back to Medical.

Onah/critter is waiting for me, a dark little lump in the glow of the torch.

'Where are we going?' The words echo, bouncing forever, and in them I hear the real question: how far are you going to make me crawl?

Onah doesn't answer, just turns around and scuttles into the darkness, like the tube is a highway and not a constrictor, squeezing me into a Kuma sausage.

It's not even crawling really, more like an endless, single elbow-scraping belly flop down the longest, most boring slide in the history of creation. I'm sure Creation would disagree with that, but it's not here right now, trying to ignore the sense of being swallowed by a metallic snake. There's no fug though. Not a skerrick or a hint, not even a mouldy, greasy whiff. In fact, there's nothing in the duct, not even dust or a hint of critter fluff. It's almost like the duct's been scoured of anything that wasn't metal. It should make me feel better, that on a deck so thick with the stuff, there's a few places free of the fug, and yet... and yet there's this uneasy sensation at my nape, stirring the hairs, that whispers that this isn't right, that I'm missing something.

It seems like I've been crawling/belly flopping for an age before I see it, and then, yeah, that uneasiness gives way to a wave of vomit. Keeping it in should be considered heroic. The scoured, clean smell of the duct gives way to charred fur and meat. That alone is enough to stir my stomach, but it's the curled, blackened husks of critters that has acid scouring my throat.

Onah/critter hops through them like they're not there. I start to crawl/belly slide back the way I've come, and for the first time notice the clean line of what I thought was black metal that appears in my wake. Vomit coats my tongue. I hold it back a second time.

Onah/critter is staring at me. I can't see his face, except in my mind, where he regards me with all four eyes, saying nothing. He doesn't have to.

I stop my backwards slide. 'What happened?'

Come.

'But the critters...'

It will not affect you.

It's tough to tell if he means the psychological damage of realising I've been slithering through the charred remains of Dude's brethren, or if whatever turned them into a crisp won't affect me. I'm not sure I want to know which, but I find myself sliding forward once more. I wish I'd grabbed a helmet, because now I know what I'm crawling through, I'm imagining it in my lungs. Critter particles in my mouth. I don't know if it's better than fug. At least the critters are dead. Carbon particles.

The first CRUNCH brings back the vomit, and this time there's no stopping it. Bile and the remnants of the protein bar I choked down spray over the duct, dribbling down my chin and neck. It mixes with the corpses on either side of me, the one I just crushed under my elbow.

'Onah...'

I don't know what I expect him to do, to offer. It's clear he wants me to do something, *needs* me to do something, and if it's got anything to do with saving *Citlali* and all the people on her, saving Grea, I'm not going to argue. But this, this is...

Onah slips into the back of my mind, his white/black presence spreading under my scalp, taking control of my arms, pulling me forward. CRUNCH. CRUNCH. CRUNCH.

I feel the skeletons pop under my elbow, the warmth as I slide over the vomit, the vile acidic stench of it mixing with the char, but it's softened, hidden behind a wall of white/black. He stays for a few moments, and underneath his presence, I sense the ugly stain of the fug, the effort it takes for him to help me. The fear under his confidence.

He leaves, and then it's only me crawling through crispy critters, but I've got it now. The distance to keep going, to ignore what used to be here, the imagined screams of the critters as whatever turned them to carbon swept through the duct.

At least it wasn't fug. Right?

And then I'm not wondering because there's a scream from ahead, the acrid scent of burnt hair and a duct-wide sheet of angry orange rushing toward me.

'Onah!'

It will not affect you.

Except it's turned the critter to ash and it's coming at me in a wave of fury and heat.

I scoot backward, but I can't move fast enough. Not. Fast. Enough.

The sheet washes over me. A tingle of energy and then it's gone. I open my eyes. I'm still here. Still flesh and shipsuit. I hold my hands up, spread my fingers. All there. All fleshy.

Onah's gone. I can't sense his presence anymore. Maybe the critter was anchoring him? It's a cinder now, and I reckon I could go back to the med bay and not have to drag myself through this graveyard, except there's a new glimmer at the end of the duct. My heart seizes and for a moment I wonder if whatever kind of security or sanitation or... whatever protocol that screen was, has recalibrated and is coming back for a Kuma-cleansing.

But the light isn't right. It's white and... is that an opening?

I slide forward, taking a moment to find that place Onah showed me before I squirm through the still-smouldering corpse of the critter, and tumble out of the duct.

For a heartbeat it's dark, and then the room lights up.

My head's still ringing from the fall, new flamethrowers are going off in my shoulder and my back is screaming at me, objecting to the hard edge that broke my tumble as I get to my feet.

Like the duct and Med, there's no fug in here that I can see. There's no wondering where I am, not with that round desk in the centre of the room, the sloping floor or the giant gold head hovering in the centre.

Command.

I'm in the centre of the ship, not physically but metaphorically. This is where all the important stuff happens, where the decisions are made. And that chair, the one sitting above all the others behind its own slice of the pie-like table, that's where Captain Lyn should sit, and there, on her right, the XO. The Chief Med would be on her other side and then Ops and Science and—

I stop thinking. Every chair reminds me of Captain's clawed hand reaching out of the goo, of the skeletal figures and fug that I pretended not to see. And every memory, *every* memory peels back the lid across the pit at the core of my soul, battered and ragged after crawling through ash and bones.

I vaguely realise I'm wiping my hands down the front of my suit, trying to get the ash out of my pores, then I hit the vomit. I jerk my hands away from my body, holding them out, wondering if the grey sludge is in any way better than the shit on my face. The smell hits me. Carbon and the rich, acid tang of vomit wriggling up my nose make my eyes water and a new round of nausea rises from my gut.

Light pierces my eyes.

I throw up my arms.

'Shut it off!'

'Kuma Darzi. You are not authorised to be here.' Core's voice booms, and now I'm covering my ears instead of my eyes, turning my head away from the drone trying to blind me.

In that half-second of blindness, something unfurls deep in my brain, bringing with it the musty scent of feathers and the soft growl of rucnart.

I lose a moment somewhere, because suddenly my vision's clear and I'm across the deck, hands on the central console. I'm not entirely sure what's happening or what I'm doing, but that thing at the back of my brain is sending instructions to my fingers and—

Electricity rips through my body, clenching muscles, my jaw locking up so tight I'm almost positive my teeth are going to shatter. Then I'm on the deck, breath coming in gasps, arms and legs and stomach still twitching from the shock.

Core's disembodied head floats over me.

'What...' I gasp the words out as the air makes it back into my lungs. 'Was... that?'

'A security protocol. You were accessing restricted systems.'

'But I didn't...' I start to say that I don't know any of the restricted systems, at least the ones serious enough to get me zapped. Then I remember the thing unfurling in my brain and...

Onah. The command sphere.

'Kuma, are you well?'

No. No, I'm not. 'What systems?' I ask.

'I cannot say. The information is restricted.'

I don't really hear that last part; all I hear is she can't say.

Can't share.

Can't ask.

Can't. Can't. Can't.

There are questions, lots and lots of questions piling up in where the kins' command sphere was, but they're not going any further. The front part of my brain is too busy trying to decide whether or not I should be finding a nice corner to curl up in a ball and finish freaking the fuck out.

Slowly, muscles still shaking, I get to my feet.

'Kuma Darzi.'

'The captain's dead.' That's the first thought that comes out of my mouth. Great.

'I know.'

'And my sister's trapped in her pod, and I can't—'

'I am aware.'

'—p'Endr's dead and there's something eating the ship—'

'Kuma Darzi.'

'—and I crawled through my own vomit, and—'

'STOP!'

I'm not sure if it's the sound or the way the sudden absence of light stops the tumble of words.

Or maybe, just maybe, it's Core standing in front of me, holographic hands on my shoulders.

'Stop, Kuma. I am aware of the situation.'

I open my mouth, but instead of words I take in a shuddering breath.

'You know?'

'Yes.'

'But, you haven't done anything.'

'I do not have access to my sub-systems.'

'The fug cut you off.'

'Indirectly. I cut myself off.'

'Why?'

'The invader has infected the system.'

'Ag.'

'Yes.'

I nod, take a step back so Core's hands are no longer fuzzing where they intersect with my shoulders. I breathe deep and cross my arms, stop as the relocated one sends shards of pain through my back, and wrap them around my middle instead, like that can hold in all the panic in my chest.

Another breath, and maybe, *maybe*, if I squeeze my arms tighter and concentrate on the pain, I can shove the hysteria into a little box and think for a second.

Core knows, she knows everything, or most of everything. That means we can fix it. That *has* to mean we can fix it. But first, I have to know one thing…

'What happened?'

The holo above the console changes, Core replaced by a spinning map of our part of the galaxy. The thumb-sized spheres of stars glowed in an endless cloud, spinning outwards from the bright yellow ball at their centre. Jørn.

Five different coloured lines wind through the holo, branching out from Jørn into different corners of the galaxy, each one a gigantic two-hundred and sixty-year-long loop that never intersected with the others. *Citlali's* journey is mapped in yellow, snaking toward the galaxy's core and back again. I step closer.

Two-thirds of the line is a solid yellow, the distance we had already travelled, the rest is dotted, showing the journey still to take. I'd be born in the Merclides system, sixty-seven years into the journey, and fifty years from here. It used to weird me out to think like that, but now? Well, now I have fug.

There's a pause. I'm waiting for Core to say something, to tell me what she found, but she's staring at the map, expression as blank as only an AI's can be.

'And?'

Core turns to me. 'And what, Kuma?'

'What did you find?'

'I have been unable to determine.'

There's another pause. It takes me a heartbeat of returning Core's stare before I realise it's not actually a pause. She stopped speaking.

Frustration and urgency make me want to vibrate right out of the room. 'Determine what?'

'What is sending the signal.' Core blinks and I swear I can see an Old Terran lightbulb going off in her head. 'Do you require more information?'

'Yes.' My hands are up in the air and anger has me stomping around the console, my boots *CLOMP CLOMP CLOMPING* on the deck. Frustration is bubbling in my chest, bursting out of my throat in a torrent of words. 'Lots more information. *All* of the information. Why'd you stop? What's eating the ship? How'd it get here? Where'd it come from?'

Core opens her mouth, but my hands are up in the air again and I'm continuing my storm around Command. 'Ag's crazy, you know. I *felt* her Core, felt her *emote*.' I pause long enough to slap my hands on the console and glare at Core. 'How does an AI *emote*, Core? It's not possible, and yet I *felt* her. Malice thick enough to choke on, filling the air like smoke.'

Core's mouth opens again, but I'm on a roll now, all the weirdness of the last few days spewing out of me. 'And the Jørans think some kind of furry, pale squash-nosed aliens are coming after us. The ones who built the under-mountain things on Jørn? Those ones. They're positive *They're* coming after us for revenge, because the water-kin did their mind-squishy thing to them way back when. Except it's not them that are eating the ship, it's some kind of fug, or space mould or... or... I don't know.'

I stop. I need to breathe. There's suddenly not enough air and my lungs are burning, demanding I gulp all the remaining oxygen down my throat. There's a wobble in my legs as well, and my knees are yelling at me to sit down, reminding me the nano-meds haven't finished working their magic. I lean on the console, putting all my weight on my hands, staring down at the pearlescent surface under them. White and clean and smooth, like it's meant to be. No fug, no holes, no dead critters, except for the ones still coating my arms and the creases between my fingers. Except for those.

Something bumps into the back of my legs, a gentle push above my knees, and I sit. Instead of landing on the floor, my butt hits a cushioned seat and I sink into the hover-chair, the jelly finally abandoning my legs.

'Mid-way through our journey to the Thorum systems, sensor's detected a signal. As per protocol, I stopped to determine if I should wake crew to investigate and sent several long-range drones to take more detailed readings,' Core said.

Above the console, the map is replaced by a complex sensor scan, the lines, dots and arcs of colour rotating slowly. 'I lost contact with the drones shortly after they reached the strongest part of the signal, but I was able to determine that it is not a natural phenomenon. The pattern is regular, although the algorithm is not with my datapaks. I can surmise that it is language, but not what it means. The fug, as you call it, is not organic but biological.' The display changes and now there's something I can recognise, the grey-green strands of the mould.

Core continues. 'I first detected it on the ship several days after I lost contact with the drones. A trace of its origin points to the signal, but is not definitive. Initial attempts to clear the infection appeared successful. Unfortunately, such was not the case. The fug had invaded several key systems before I was aware of the danger.'

'Why didn't you wake the crew?'

'I did, Kuma. The first system to fail was stasis/sleep.'

'It's meant to be the most protected.'

'I do not have answers, I can only tell you what happened. I was able to rouse the captain, but not fully.'

'She's dead. So's the Executive Officer and Chief Med. And p'Endr.' I'm remembering them as I say their names.

'I see.'

'No, you don't.' She hadn't even known the captain was dead, that her kids were dead too, and it's that thought, that memory, that makes me angry. 'You cut yourself off. There's a forcefield around your processing core and nothing anywhere else. The fug ate through the stasis units, made holes big enough to crawl through. *I* saw the captain, saw her hand clawing through the stasis gel. Except it wasn't gel anymore, it was some kind of mouldy, hard shit and she *died* in it.'

I'm breathing hard again, leaning forward in the chair and gripping the armrests. Core's expression flickers between seriousness and concern, like she can't quite make up her mind which emotion she should be faking.

In the end, she goes with neither.

'The fug appears to be a bio-metallic compound, similar to nanotechnology except... not. I do not have a better explanation, Kuma. Without access to Lab or Medical or the crew, I cannot give you a definitive answer. The fug is a biological metallic entity similar in composition to nanites. In effect, it is a lifeform.'

'And it's eating us because...?'

'It is not *eating* the *Citlali*. It is breaking it down and transferring the materials back to its origin.'

'The signal?'

'That is my conclusion.'

'But why?'

'I do not know.'

I'm so sick of all the things I don't know. All of the things I can't *do*. I can't get Grea out of her pod, can't wake Jim Engineer, can't save p'Endr. I can't reach across the void and take all the answers from the intelligence on the other end of the fug—

A light goes off in my head. 'The fug was in the eter.' I'd picked it up, pulled it apart and sensed the intelligence *behind* it before Onah pulled me out.

'Technology is not capable of psionics, Kuma.'

'You said it was biological.' Excitement makes my blood fizz and puts the stuffing back in my bones.

'I need fug.'

CHAPTER FOURTEEN

It's not as easy to get fug as you would think. For one, Core didn't want to let me out of Command, and she sealed the duct to make sure I couldn't escape. It took me an hour, a plan and a lot of diagrams to convince her to let me crawl back through the ash-stained duct, and I had a tail as I did so. A drone the size of my fist shot out of the centre console and followed me. It was comforting, even if it felt like Core was staring at me the whole time. At least there weren't any vibes coming off her like Ag.

I tumbled out into Med with the same grace as I'd done it at the other end, which is to say I landed on my head. Somehow, I managed to roll into it, taking the brunt of the fall on my shoulder, the injured one 'cause I'm lucky like that. At least there was the mountain of furniture to make the descent a little easier, but that didn't stop the pain ripping through my back or the half-scream from my lips.

The med bots descended like a flock of angry qwans, armed with pink nano-meds. Needless to say, the next six hours weren't fun, but at the end of it, my knees didn't scream at me and neither did my shoulder.

Gotta love nano-meds.

Then came the plan.

Core supplied the blueprints, Med supplied the equipment and I followed their instructions. And scolding, until finally I heft a new and improved Franken-thrower.

Getting out of Med was the next hard part.

We can't just open the door and grab some fug. There's the barrier for one, and there's something wrong with the door mechanism. The fug's probably eaten it. So Core's taking me the back way.

The back way is another air duct, as tight as the first but without the coating of soot. Or the bodies. There's also a distinct lack of oxygen. Which is the bad news; I'm wearing an envirosuit's helmet, and that turns the already tight tube into a Kuma-shaped sock. The helmet's a little too big, and while it's not scraping the sides, if I lift my head too high there's this dull THUD and jerk at the back of my neck. So I'm sliding along with my head down and the only way I can see where I'm going is by rolling my eyeballs as far up as they'll go.

It's giving me a headache, but I can't quite bring myself to stare at my hands and let the drone guide me.

'How much farther?'

'Thirteen metres until the junction.'

'And how much farther after that?'

'It's is not far, Kuma Darzi.'

'That's what you said at the last junction.'

'And it is still correct.'

'You're not the one crawling through a duct, hauling a jerry-rigged flamethrower behind him.'

There's no answer to that.

I guess it wasn't really a question.

Thirteen metres seems like a gazillion when you're commando-crawling through a duct barely big enough for your elbows, but sure enough, the junction is right there – a t-shaped intersection of yet more square tubes even smaller than the one I'm in. The drone disappears down the right one and I spend a few minutes wondering how I'm going to squeeze myself around the corner, let alone manoeuvre the mammoth length of the Franken around after me, when the duct disappears from under me.

Two things. One, I'm glad I'm wearing the helmet and two, it's not far to fall, but I really wish it were.

I'm caught in fug. Like. Caught.

Belly-down, faceplate to grey-green wavy shit, the Franken on my back. I'm caught up in some kind of tangle of vines. Through the arm-thick strands, I can see decking and the fug-eaten sides of a corridor.

I reckon the fug is as surprised as I am.

And then just like that, it drops me.

'Oh shit.'

I don't know where the vid-star moves come from, but I'm pretty sure I've never moved so fast in my life. One moment I'm falling, the next I'm kneeling on the deck, one fist to the floor as the other swings the Franken around. I'm picturing Dude, standing on an island made of the old Franken back on Lab Two, imagining him pulling his ninja moves, as I push to my feet and set the corridor ablaze.

Fug screams but the helmet muffles the sound, and watching the way the stuff shrivels and turns to ash brings with it an unpleasant glee, bubbling up from inside like a particularly sick volcano. It doesn't seem like me, but then it does and I lose myself to the sensation, swinging the Franken around like a firehose. A fiery, fire hose. The glee chuckles.

It takes the drone bobbing in front of my face, getting in the way of my fire-throwing party, to bring me back to myself.

I'm not where I started, and all around me is the blackened remnants of fug, curled up and desiccated where they aren't piles of soot and char.

Shit. The command sphere. Still sitting in my brain. What had Onah wanted me to do?

It's not a question for now. Now that I've stopped blasting it with flame, the fug is making a comeback, the vines gathering like a wave, ready to launch their next assault. I grab a sample of new grey-green fug from amongst the ash, ripping it from the wall. It peels off with a reluctant tearing sound, and I slap it into the container attached to my arm. The container lights up, a mini containment field encircling it the moment the lid is sealed.

Here's hoping the field and plasglas slow the fug down.

And then I'm out of there.

Crawling back through the duct is as bad as going the other way, but somehow it seems longer, what with the fug thrashing around in its container on my arm. The Franken slides along after me: *scrape, scrape, shussh*. And then I'm tumbling down another mountain of furniture, this time without the finesse of the vid star. The Franken crashes into my arse, and I sprawl on the deck as a med drone bobs an inch from my face, slim arms extending to take the fug from my arm.

It's done and gone before I right myself, the drone whisking the container to the glowing circle at the centre of the ring of med beds. A column rises from the floor and the drone places the container on the top. It's barely set it down before a forcefield encloses the container. Seems like Med isn't taking any chances.

As another handful of drones pop out of the wall, I take a moment to check in on Dude. The sides of the med unit are transparent now. He's not so fluffy anymore, or golden. Sometime during his stay in the box, Med gave him a shave, transforming him from a cute ball of fuzz to a sleek black-skinned predator, with a short, sharp snout and six paws almost as big as his head. I never noticed that before, or how big his eyes were, or the fine points of fangs peeking from beneath his top lip.

Makes me wonder what genes the engineers mixed together and why.

There's no time to ponder it now though. Core/drone is hovering in the corner of my vision. AIs don't do impatience, or at least, that's what everyone's always said, but they also said they couldn't emote, and I swear Core/drone is vibrating.

I'm being herded to the nearest med bed. Me playing mental footsies with the fug has both Med and Core/drone on edge, or maybe it's because they have nothing else to do so they're hovering like a flock of nervous qwans.

I settle cross-legged on the med bed, take a deep breath and focus on the fug. It writhes within the container, the single tendril smacking the plasglas again and again and again. I close my eyes, carrying the picture of the fug with me as I slip into the eter.

The Med lab is gone. There's nothing here but me and the endless white, not even my own shadow. A deep breath. I reach out, using the image of the fug as a guide, and there it is, a breath away. I *pull*. The eter shivers and I'm not alone anymore. The tendril sits before me, a finger-length of grey-green swaying back and forth like it's waving at me. I concentrate.

I'm not sure if I get smaller or the fug gets bigger, but one moment it's a speck in the eter and the next it's everything, the grey-green surrounding me, and amongst it, the sparkling veins of red. I focus harder and the red dissolves, becoming the sharp snap of silver and an intelligence that evades my senses and yet...

And yet.

It's the yet I'm after, the possibility, the hint of something other hiding behind the silver. I plunge into it.

The river from before takes me, plunging me into a maelstrom of silver and red. And there's that sensation again, of the threads of reality parting, and I'm watching them. Tiny slivers of impossible, bits of chaos, of *everything* barely bigger than a molecule, and then bigger and then—

I sense Onah before I see him. The white/black presence is beside me, reaching out, trying to pluck me from the rapids. Fear rides on the tips of his talons. Raw and hot, brushing against my neck, raising the hairs even as it causes a confusion of images to bloom in my mind. AD Tudor is dancing beside *Them*, their flat noses pressed up against his chest while the beacon flashes and pulses in the background. And then there's blood, human and *Theirs*, running down my throat, staining fur and feathers. Trees falling, chicks crushed and mangled. Despair. Ancient and powerful, echoing through the generations. I rip myself out of the memories.

I twist, evading Onah's grasp. He reaches again. I dive deeper, seeking out the rips, plunging my fingers into the holes, ripping, stretching, and all the while Onah is behind me, reaching, reaching, reaching. His talons scrape my skin.

I pull. The rip gets bigger, seems to reach back for me.

And then Onah's gone and I'm... I'm...

Where am I?

This is not the Aer. The river and endless white have been replaced by darkness. Not the too-personal darkness of Onah's eter, filled to the brim with kin hiding in shadow. This appears empty. Formless. But it's not mine. It's not anyone's. I don't know how I know that. Maybe it's the feeling, like hanging in the midst of the void, alone except for distant stars, and even that isn't right, doesn't quite encompass the sensation of waiting, of possibility. Anything can happen here. That sense blooms in my chest.

Anything.

But it's not the everything that I sensed in the river. Where is the knowledge, the promise of *knowing*?

I feel like I've been slapped in the face. There's nothing here. Nothing and—

Wait. I twist around. There *is* something. Behind me, a weird little shiver over my skin, except it's not so little, raising goosebumps up and down my arms. And suddenly I'm picturing myself in Dad's lab, but this time there's a creeping chill running over my body, the same sense of being repulsed that I felt from the disc in the wall. It's stronger here, and it's coming from behind me, from *Citlali*.

AD was right. It *is* a beacon.

And something's answering it.

I twist back around.

There's nothing to see, only the same electric shiver of intent I saw within the fug.

Is that what I sensed before? Is that what's hiding behind the fug?

A piece of the darkness moves, or does something move *in* the darkness? It's hard to tell. There's no light to see by, and yet...

It's a ripple masquerading as sight, fooling my senses. I guess my brain has no reference for what it's experiencing and so the movement whispers against my skin, shivers down my bones. I sense the thing out there, and it's more than witnessing it with my eyes, or touching it. It's all of my senses wrapped up into one with the added something of my empathic abilities. I *experience* the being, the weight of its thoughts, the slow, bleary beat of its consciousness, muffled under a heavy kind of sleep. Heavier than stasis, heavier than anything I've ever sensed. It's like death, except that's not right. It's the moment *before* death. Like the weight that invaded p'Endr's bones as she breathed her last, the darkness that clouded her vision, the stone that stilled her heart. Whatever is out there, it's asleep and not quite dead.

Death sleep.

It's dying. The thing is dying. Why? How?

I will myself toward it, but no matter how hard I propel myself, how fast I move, how far, it never gets any closer. Always a whisper against my skin. Sleeping and yet not.

I need answers. I *came* here for answers. I need them to stop the fug, and the thing has them, is the *everything* I came for.

I can't leave until I have answers. I *won't* leave.

There's no time in this place, or at least, I don't think there's any time. It's strange, there and not, like my sight. I chase the thing for an eternity, and yet it's a moment as well, a heartbeat. I don't feel hunger or fatigue, but I sense myself growing weaker, like I'm fading. I take a moment to rest. To think, to try. Chasing the thing isn't working. I have to be smarter.

My thoughts are like fairy floss, thin and fluffy, shredding before I get hold of them. It takes effort – a long slow second to form a thought but only a moment for it dissolve. And now I'm wondering why I'm trying. What was I doing? What's the presence out there in the dark?

I chase it. I have to know.

Something, not the thing I'm chasing but another thing, breaches the darkness behind me. Pain laces my body.

The void is gone. I open my eyes to soft grey and a bright red flash. My brain is mushy. It takes a moment and another flash before I recognise the slow glide of a scanner passing over me, and the contours of a ceiling.

The Med lab.

I'm on my back. The pain that ripped me out of that place is gone. In its place is a heaviness I haven't felt before, like all the marrow has been scooped out of my bones and the hollows filled with steelcrete. I try to sit up.

I get as far as lifting my head before blackness pulls at the edge of my vision.

When I try opening my eyes again, Dude's sitting on my forehead. He *fuzzes*.

Hey, little guy. Wait. That was wrong. I meant to say that, so where are the words?

Confusion is muddying my brain. I'm missing something, something more than the warmth in my bones.

There's a hiss, a cool *shh-stick* in my neck. I turn my head to see a med bot, a hypo in one of its arms, before darkness takes me again.

Being drugged isn't fun, which is probably why I bitch-slap the med drone the moment it comes near me. The thing hits the floor and I'm pretty sure I hear plasform crack.

Thankfully, I can get up this time around. My back is a solid ache, doing as much to get me to my feet as the thought of the horde of med drones probably coming for me right this nano-second.

I spin around.

Nothing, just the one drone, slowly picking itself off the deck. It's not big, about the size of my fist, and egg-shaped. It hovers, a spot lighting up on the rounded point of its nose before a scan snaps out of it, the fan of red passing over me, head to toe and back.

The light snaps off and the drone darts back into its dock in the wall.

I relax, but only by an iota, and take stock.

I'm in the Med lab, in the exact same spot I sat to venture into the void, but the place seems different. Or maybe that's the way I smell?

I lift my arm to check.

Whoa. There must be something wrong with my shipsuit, because I could knock myself out with that odour. Then again…

'Med?' My voice comes out as a thin whisper of sound, and it feels like my vocal cords are clogged up. I clear my throat and try again. 'Med, how long was I out?'

The AI's blue face appears in front of me. 'You have been unconscious for seventeen days and sixteen hours.'

I mustn't have heard that right. 'Seventeen *days*?'

'Indeed. After thirty-six hours of mental communication, your vital signs became critical and I was forced to administer electric shocks to sever the connection. After which I deemed it necessary to enforce an extended period of recuperation.'

I remember the hypo-stick and translate "enforced recuperation" to mean induced coma. And now I'm remembering chasing the *thing*, of pushing myself further and further, how my thoughts turned to taffy, and that sense of fading.

It's not that I'd chased the *thing* for so long and so far that I'd almost died, that make my insides go cold. It's the realisation of how very far that was, and how much farther the *thing* was, the distance between us.

And I'd sensed it.

I push myself off the bed. My legs wobble for a moment, before holding steady.

A med bot hovers in front of me, and another next to my shoulder. I have the sense that if I so much as lean the wrong way, they'll "enforce recuperation" again.

Let them try.

I need to save Grea. What's happened to her in seventeen days? Is she huddled up in her pod? Is she still breathing? Or is she like

Captain Lyn, stuck in stasis gel, reaching for air?

But even if I go down there, storm the stasis unit with Franken-thrower and Dude, what am I going to do? How am I going to pull her out, and what about Mum and Dad and Jim Engineer?

I need answers. I'd reached through the fug to get them, found some*thing* else and almost died.

Mum, Dad, Grea, even dying doesn't change anything, except what I do next.

CHAPTER FIFTEEN

Shuttle bays are just big airlocks. That thought pops into my head as I stand in front of the one on Ag deck, wishing for something a little more substantial than my shipsuit to protect me. I remember standing in this very spot, rolling my eyes as Dad double-checked the seals on my envirosuit.

'We're in the outer hull, kiddo, only the ice hull and thirty centimetres of steelcrete between us and space.' He'd tugged on my helmet, almost pulling my head off my shoulders.

'I need my head, Dad.'

He'd bopped me on said head, his fist *THUNKING* on my helmet's plasform. 'A micro-fracture in the hull is all it takes, kiddo, and you're breathing vacuum.'

I'd rolled my eyes again. 'You can't *breathe* in vacuum, Dad. There's no air.'

His face had turned grim, the skin around his eyes tightening, his mouth firming. 'Exactly,' he'd said. He'd turned away but in that second, I'd caught a rush of emotion rolling off him in a black wave of grief.

The memory of it hit me in the gut. I hadn't asked him about it then, or later. I'd asked Mum, but she'd got that same expression on her face and said she'd tell me some day. An echo of Dad's emotions had rolled off her before she'd caught it. She'd never told me what caused it but I didn't really need the details anymore. I recognised that particular, piercing shade of darkness, caught a shadow of it every time I imagined Grea's hand reaching out of decaying biogel.

Dude *fuzzes*, trying to comfort me.

I tilt my head enough to feel the smooth, warm glide of Dude's fur against my chin. Tension runs up and down my spine, making the hair at my nape stand on end as I try to remember where the envirosuits are.

That memory of Ag's emote is haunting the shit out of me. It's more than the fact she did it, it's the chilling menace in her eyes... if I could have crawled back up the air duct to Lab Two to access the shuttle bay there, I would have. If I'd thought I could shoot myself out an airlock and *swim* to the source of the fug, I'd have done that too, anything but stand here and test my memory of Ag's expression.

But I can't do any of those things.

I breathe deep and punch the door controls.

If Ag wants to suck me out into space, she's going to have to be quick about it.

The shuttle bay is cold enough my breath frosts on the air, which isn't a good sign. It should be the same temperature as the rest of the deck, pleasant enough that I'm not getting goosebumps under my shipsuit. The only light comes from the hallway, and it throws my shadow across the grated decking, all the way to the sleek-nosed shuttle sitting in the middle of the cavernous space. Wider across than the freight tubes, its wings tucked up against its sides, the shuttle takes up most of the bay. There's enough room either side for it to lift on its thrusters and turn around.

The height of two decks, the bay is bigger vertically than it is horizontally.

I glance up, catching glimpses of the catwalks overhead and the framework where the other EVA vehicles are stored, their bellies little more than lighter patches of grey in the darkness.

I can't see the hatch that separates the bay from the launch tunnel, it's hidden behind the shuttle and smothered in darkness. I'm safe so long as the internal doors are open, or at least that's the theory, but in theory the captain should have been safe in her stasis unit and Ag shouldn't been able to emote.

The spare envirosuits are in a locker along one side of the shuttle bay, or at least they should be. Somewhere between Onah pushing me out of stasis/sleep and learning about the beacon, I've stopped believing in the way things *should* be.

A light comes on over the shuttle. A drone hovers over its nose, shedding light like a miniature sun.

'Ag? Is that you?'

It blinks.

I take that as a yes.

Ice slithers down my spine while I try to get an eye on the suit lockers.

The drone dips and zooms toward the back of the shuttle, away from the inner doors.

Okay. To follow or not to follow? If I go deeper into the bay, I stand less chance of making it out to the safety of the corridor if Ag loses her shit.

The fact that I'm not sensing anything from Ag is what decides for me. As far as my psyche is concerned, it's just me and Dude up here, playing chicken in the dark.

I follow the drone.

I'm halfway around the shuttle, half my attention on the drone while the rest of me eyeballs the envirosuit lockers. I've decided that I can reach one and drag a suit out before Ag opens the outer hatch by more than a few centimetres, long enough to slam a helmet over my head. I might even get a leg on and be able to active the mag boots before the out-rush of air drags me across the deck.

Dude'll have to hang on though and he might not make it.

Surreptitiously, I bring up my palm unit and make a few modifications to my shipsuit. There's a tingle over my chest as the nano-fabric adjusts itself, a few seconds and when it's done my sleeves are up around my elbows, but there's an expanded Dude-sized pouch over my heart.

The drone has stopped by the shuttle's tail. It's hovering at head height, waiting for me.

Casually, I shift Dude from my shoulder to the pouch.

The slow *shushing* sound doesn't immediately register in my brain. It's coming from the shuttle bay doors. Not the inner ones, the ones that lead to the rest of the ship, but the outer ones. The ones that lead to vacuum.

I'm across the decking before my head has time to identify the sound. The locker is under my hand, the panel sliding aside. I grab the suit first, thrusting one leg in, activating the mag boots, just as I planned, before I realise that the outer door isn't moving. A quick check over my shoulder and yep, the inner doors are open as well.

The drone is bobbing over my head, helpfully directing light into the locker and lighting up the space around me so I don't have to guess what part of the suit I'm shoving my other leg into.

I look directly at the drone and frown. If I was trying to space someone, I wouldn't be so helpful.

Since I'm half in anyway, I finish putting the suit on. Not speeding through it, but not dawdling either. Taking the time to make sure the seals are green and the nano-fabric adjusts to the Dude-shaped lump on my chest. I tuck the helmet under my arm. It's a larger model than the one I grabbed from Ag deck, a transparent dome of plasglas, but my thumb against the rim collapses it into a ring a centimetre thick, ready to slip over my head.

'So. You're not trying to kill me.'

The drone blinks.

'So, what are you doing?'

It zips away, back toward the rear of the shuttle, but this time, instead of hovering, it turns its light on the outer doors.

There's not much to see, at least not at this distance. I follow the drone and take another look.

The outer doors are made of the same steelcrete as the inner ones, except thicker, without the smooth off-white finish. They're bigger too, half the height of the shuttle bay and as wide. The engineers had built these two slabs of steelcrete and no one had tried to pretty them up, like someone had decided that we all needed a reminder that these doors were here to keep us safe, not comfortable.

I guess that was the reason for the big, read letters emblazoned on the deck underneath them, and again on the doors themselves. "DANGER. VACUUM."

I know. It seems kinda redundant, but people are stupid. Grea says that all the time, mostly when she's looking at me. Onah refines that, he says *humans* are stupid, and I can never quite tell if he's including Jørgens in that, or just referring to the full-humans. It doesn't really matter, because right now I've got other things to worry about, like the faint shimmer of light over the steelcrete.

Steelcrete doesn't shimmer, not on its own at least. I move a few steps closer.

It's not shimmering on its own now either. There's ice over the doors, a thick skin of it slithering outwards from what must be a micro-fracture in the hatch. What could crack steelcrete?

I lean closer, then jerk back.

Fug. There's fug in the ice, trapped in it like… like… fug in ice.

Except the fug's moving, spreading through the ice in grey-green veins. Growing, expanding… cracking the ice, splitting it, and now the soft *shush* that drew me here is sharper, louder.

'Oh shit.'

It was a good thing I was in the suit.

One moment I'm staring at a widening crack in the ice and the next, there's a gale in the shuttle bay. The sound of it drowns the wail of the siren. Whistling past my ears, pushing my hair in my face, and taking my feet out from under me.

I hit the deck back first, my head follows and stars burst in front of my eyes. Everything around me goes fuzzy, and there's a strange metallic fullness in my nose, like my brain is trying to escape out my nostrils. The blow scrambles my brain and for a moment I'm nowhere – here and yet not as it goes through a quick reset.

It's a nano-second, long enough to skid a few metres along the deck as vacuum tries to suck me out into space, along with the atmosphere. Somehow, I've managed to hold onto the envirosuit's helmet during the moment my brain was getting scrambled.

Small mercies.

I can use some of those right now.

I jam the helmet on and the dome explodes around my head. I hold my breath until I hear the *shuuuush* of oxygen.

The micro-fracture isn't so micro. There's a massive split in the steelcrete doors that separate the shuttle bay from the ice hull, and it's growing.

Now I get why the drone was blinking its circuits off.

It would really help if Ag found some working vocal circuits.

I wait until my boots hit the doors before activating the mag circuits.

There's no way I can hear it over the noise of escaping atmosphere and sirens, but I imagine the *shhhtuck* sound of them sticking to the metal.

Getting up isn't as easy as it sounds. The grav is still on, and with my boots stuck to the wall the only way upright is to flip around onto my belly and push myself off the deck.

I'm glad I'm wearing the helmet.

I hit the bulkhead hard, and even with the plasteel protecting my head, stars burst again in front of my eyes and my brain resets for the second time.

It resets pretty fast, a blink, which is just as well 'cause I'm staring at a crate rocketing toward my face.

Shit.

I throw myself to the side, the crate embeds itself right where my face used to be.

Shit.

Adrenalin shuts off the front part of my brain. There's screaming in there; blind panic leaving no room to reason, to survive.

I can feel it behind the wall of neuro-chemicals, but it can't reach me. I have the unpleasant idea that the neuro-chems are like the ice over the door. They're going to crack soon enough, and once they do, it'll be bye-bye Kuma. The thought dumps more adrenalin into my system.

Rational thought is trapped somewhere between the gibbering panic and the chems. It's instinct as much as the knowledge embedded in my brain by a lifetime of emergency drills that guide me now.

The inner bay doors are still open. If I can get to them and hit the emergency close, I'll be fine. Except walking across the deck is like trying to climb a mountain in a tornado. The air wants out, and it's taking every loose thing with it. Tools and envirosuits, even a fuzz-ball a little too much like a critter for my comfort, comes whizzing at me. I never knew there was so much stuff in this section of Ag, and it's all aimed at my head.

'Ag! Shut the inner doors!'

Nothing happens. It was worth a try.

A look up confirms that the vehicles suspended overhead are moving too. Not in an insane, Kuma-killing way, but a gentle sway that nonetheless gives the panicked, gibbering part of my brain another reason to squeal in terror and wonder if getting crushed by a maintenance bot would hurt.

Thanks brain. Really didn't need that.

The only thing that's not moving is the shuttle.

If I can get to it, I'll be safe.

Safe.

That's the only thought the not-gibbering part of me needs.

I duck and weave my way across the deck to the shuttle.

It takes longer than it should, but a check of my chrono reveals it's only been a few minutes since the ice cracked and unleashed hell.

Once in the lee of a landing strut, the tornado lessens and I'm able to stand upright. I pray the fug hasn't gotten to the shuttle and slap the lighter patch of hull on its belly.

The square lights up from within and a corresponding rectangle glows on the shuttle's belly, and a long narrow ramp pops out and clanks onto the deck. I'm up the ramp in seconds, into the tiny confines of the airlock.

The door snaps shut behind me.

Silence. It's hard to realise how loud the gale is until you're out of it.

There's a faint ringing in my ears, and the ragged sound of my breathing seems loud, too loud, but not loud enough to drown out the pounding of my heart. Or the *shoosh* of the inner airlock cycling open and the *clank* as the gangway retracts into the hull.

The strength goes out of my legs at the same moment the crying, screaming, gibbering part of my brain breaks through the adrenalin.

I don't know how long I've sat in the airlock, but my eyes hurt and my nose is raw from wiping it on my sleeve.

Somewhere in the storm of crazy, enough sense broke through for me to collapse the helmet. I reckon it was around the time Dude squeezed through the collar and threatened to suffocate me by curling under my nose.

I feel old. Everything is heavy, my head, my heart, my feet. I can do something about my feet by turning the mag-boots off. The rest of me… I sniff and wipe my nose a final time.

The only way out is through, or at least, that's what Mum says.

The thought of Mum makes my throat close up again and brings the burn of tears to my eyes but I push it back and get to my feet.

The cockpit is through the main cabin, a big open space stuffed with equipment. The cockpit is separated from the cabin by the backs of two flight chairs. The space lights up at my approach, first the glows in the floor and the spine of the shuttle, then the cockpit itself.

There are no windows, the hull's stronger when it doesn't have holes in it, and so when the cockpit lights up, it's not just with the glows you see by.

The curved expanse of dull grey steelcrete that forms the nose of the shuttle is there one moment and gone the next. In its place is the shuttle bay.

I slip into a flight chair and take stock

Sometime during my breakdown, the bay's inner doors closed, killing the tornado.

The shuttle is a miniature version of the *Citlali,* with all the same scanners, meant to take the crew where the bigger ship can't go. Moons and asteroids, even atmosphere, all of the things that *Citlali* is too big to survive. The best thing about it? There's no fug.

The shuttle AI boots right up.

It's not the same AI as *Citlali,* not even a fragment, and it's nice to see a different face hovering over the console, even if it looks like it sucked a lemon. Narrowed eyes and pursed lips, and that wasn't even shuttle's angry face. Not that he's capable of angry, his face is stuck like that.

I clear my throat and wipe my nose.

'Shuttle, prep for flight.'

There's a shiver of power, more felt than heard, and a holographic, head-sized sphere appears in my lap. The shuttle's control sphere.

I sink my hands into the light, spread fingers sliding in up to the knuckles. You can't hear the engines roar, but I imagine I can as the shuttle lifts off the deck.

A slow twist of my hands engages the thruster and a grid overlays the canopy as we start to rotate. There are distances, scans and readouts popping up around each new item, the information fading to the background when my eye passes over them without stopping.

Then the big outer doors are coming into view, "DANGER. VACUUM." blazing red over the screen, another smaller blaze joining it as the scanners pick up the micro-fracture.

I ignore it.

The outer doors open.

If you were expecting to see stars through the widening gap, you'd be disappointed. I mean, there are stars out there, but they're not *right* there, like on the other side of the doors. I've got to make it through the ice hull first.

I lift my hands within the control sphere and the shuttle rises off the deck; stretch my fingers and feel the kick as the rear thrusters engage, propelling us forward.

It always gets me how big the shuttle is when you're in it. The nose passes through the bay doors and it seems like the wings are going to scrape the sides of the tunnel. I know it's not, because there aren't any warnings blaring in my face and the readouts tell me I'm three metres clear on all sides, but still there's sweat trickling down my spine, and I'm in danger of biting through my lip.

It gets worse on the other side of the hatch, in the ice tunnel.

It's not like the tunnel is any smaller than the hatch, it's not. It's… dark, I guess. Holos light up the sides, pulses streaking past me above and below, red for starboard, white for port, blue and green for top and bottom. They're guides, there to stop me from crashing into the ice or arriving in the shuttle bay upside down. The holos don't touch the ice.

The ice isn't just black, it's a soul-devouring nothingness that makes the vacuum of space appear homey. I know I should be used to it by now – Dad took Grea and I on our first extra-*Citlali* excursion when we were two weeks old – but there's always been something about the ice hull, something… wrong.

Now I recognise it for what it is. The beacon.

I've tried explaining it others, but they look at me like I'm stupid or delusional, or pulling some kind of long-running joke. The only other person who really gets it is Grea, although she pretends not to. Grea pretends a lot of things, that she's the smartest and the most responsible, that she doesn't believe in the same weird shit that I do. She fools a lot of people – Mum, Dad, Mac (who should know better), even herself – but she can't fool me, which pisses her off.

It doesn't change the fact that every time I go into it, all that ice makes my stomach curdle. Like there's something in there, alive and watching me. Except every time I try to find it, stretching my senses until my brain threatens to peel off the inside of my skull, all I get is the same sense of something on the edge of my understanding.

Sometimes I think, that if I could turn my brain on its side and squint, I'd see it.

I used to believe that if I could see it, it wouldn't weird me out so much. That was before I knew about the beacon.

The outer hull that I bang on inside the ship isn't really the outer hull. There are two other hulls wrapping it up like a giant onion and the thickest one is the ice hull.

It takes a lot of water to run *Citlali* and it isn't like there are any resupply stations out here because, well, no one's *been* out here before. So we had to bring it with us. Beyond the steelcrete wrapping around the habitual areas of the ship is the ice hull, a twenty-three-metre thick sheet of ice wrapped in its own steelcrete skin. It covers the *Citlali*, providing us with all the water we'll ever need and additional protection from the dangers of space.

And yeah, it's ice, not water. When the environment outside can boil/freeze your insides in ninety seconds, keeping water liquid takes energy, a *lot* of energy, and it's not like we've got a tribe of swatai swimming around in there. Or maybe we have and someone forgot? I imagine a group of small, lizard-like creatures with fins and triangular heads, frozen in the ice hull for the last hundred and twenty-three years and Jim Engineer going 'whoops'.

It'd be funny, if I didn't have training memories from the last time someone killed a tribe of Jørans.

There was no one left to say 'whoops' after that.

It seems like forever before I'm passing through the final hatch.

Where the ice hull gives me the creeps, floating out into space is like entering everything. Like that moment in the eter when it felt like I was about to slip through the fabric of reality. It's indescribable, massive. Different. Dark. Really, really dark.

I've never been in interstellar space. I mean, I *have* because the *Citlali* has to pass through it to get to the next solar system, but I've never been awake, never been *in* it, a part of it like I am now. It doesn't appear any different. I mean, there's no sun casting a shadow against the ship, no moons, no planets, just a trillion tiny pinpricks of light out there in the void. I could be in the middle of the Thorum system, except… I don't know. The void appears bigger somehow. Emptier. Colder.

If I believe Onah, somewhere out there are a horde of pale, wide-nosed aliens bent on eating us. On getting revenge.

A shiver prickles my arms, embeds itself deep in my bones. Suddenly it's quiet. A tomb. I shiver again.

I turn the shuttle around, twisting my hands in the control sphere. Somewhere out there, the thrusters are firing. If it weren't for the pinprick stars, moving like molasses, and the scanners, I wouldn't know we were moving. There's no sound, no inertia to guide me. I should be used to it by now, I know, but there's something strange about not feeling where you're going. Every time I take the controls, it's a few days before I get my space legs back. Grea takes to it like a critter to junk, like she's got vacuum in her legs or something. She can't fly atmosphere like I can though. Pity there's none here.

It's a slow-moving age before I get my first glimpse of *Citlali*. It's a slither at first, the curve of the engines coming into view and then the giant curve of the hull. It's too dark to see it with my eyes, the light from the distant suns is barely enough to cast the ship in dull shades of grey, a shade lighter than the void. It's the shuttle's scanners that do most of the work, the AI who fills the viewscreen with an image of the *Citlali*, or how it would appear under the glow of a closer sun. The ship appears the same. What I can see of it. Even with the scanners, we're too close to see the whole of the squished oval shape, thinner and pointier at the bow and rounded at the stern. A quick check shows we're three kilometres from the ship. You can't see much from three klicks out, even if there was enough light.

I let out a breath, feel tension ride out of my shoulders. I don't know what I'd been expecting, but a hole in the outer hull had been the least of it. Maybe a horde of tiny fug ships, carrying bits of the—

'What's that?' I point at a faint trail of heat snaking away from the hull.

The AI enhances the image, and now I'm not looking at a thin yellow-red ribbon of heat, I have a screen full of data and an up-close and personal view of... I lean closer, narrowing my eyes. The screen blows the image up.

There's no colour, but I recognise the tendril-like stuff floating through the vacuum. I jerk back. Fug. Forget ships, or bots. That's a fug flotilla, a barge, a hover, a sled, a... a...

Thought stops, because there aren't only pieces of the hull being carried off. The viewscreen is enhancing the scan as I watch, and as I watch my stomach is trying to crawl out my mouth. There're more than steelcrete and plasform in that trail of fug. There's blood and bone and skin.

The AI enhances the scan, building a new image from the data rushing across the screen. A face stares back at me.

I know that face.

Vomit explodes in my mouth.

I turn away from the console, spewing acid and what's left of the ration bar over the deck.

There are orange flecks in the bile sprayed across the decking. Mac used to say it was little chunks of the carrot farm growing in our belly. I used to believe him, right up until I turned five and Mum sat me down and told me about stomach lining and how carrots *really* grew. Grea pretended like it was funny, but I knew she believed Mac too. We all believed Mac.

There's a flurry against my chest, and then Dude is popping his head out of my shipsuit, making like he's going to scamper down and start on the vomit spreading across the deck. I take him out, put him down and then slowly, because my bones hurt almost as much as my heart, turn back to the viewscreen.

Mae Liu's face is still there, eyes and mouth open, like she's surprised.

'Stop!'

The viewscreen goes dark.

There's a question I have to ask, should ask, but I can't quite get my mouth around the words.

'How... how many—' I swallow. "People" makes the acid roil in my stomach. 'How many biologicals in the... the fug?'

'I do not recognise the definition of "fug".'

'The trail, the stuff, the...' I wave my hand at the viewscreen.

'Scans show several dozen biologicals in the trail. I estimate thirteen are former crew members.'

Please, let none of them be Grea.

I take my hands out of the controls. 'Follow it.'

CHAPTER SIXTEEN

The shuttle knows where it's going. We're following the trail of fug, *Citlali* getting smaller and smaller in the port-side canopy. I try not to notice it, the way it kinda zooms outwards like a holo. The holes in the hull aren't as obvious, dull blue patches on the otherwise grey hull. It's always strange, seeing *Citlali* like this. The long, blunt-nosed shape always looks weird, unexpected, like I had something else in mind. Don't ask me why, it's not like I haven't seen the ship a million times on a holo. It still hits me in the gut, the reality of it.

The shuttle keeps following the fug and eventually, the Citlali is an after-image on my eyeballs. Still, I can't help but stare out the canopy. All around me is black and cold and nothing. Except now, I'm reminded of the space beyond the eter, and instead of vacuum, I see possibilities and wonder.

A million light years away, suns burn but that light makes the darkness darker. I can't help but wonder how far away they are, how I was supposed to wake up not here, but four light years away, with the light of the Thorum system's sun recharging *Citlali's* batteries. Instead I'm here, without even an AI to keep me company.

Dude *fuzzes* and sneaks under my chin.

'Just you and me, Dude.' I bury my fingers in his fur. 'Just you and me.'

Except that's not quite true. The presence I sensed in the everything is out there, a pinprick of light in the void, brushing up against my awareness like someone switched on a light. It's not as bright as the distant stars, but it's stronger than it was, still quiet, still in something deeper than sleep but not quite a coma. It grows stronger the farther along the trail we go, not because it's waking but because we're getting closer.

The shuttle's sensors beep and a map overlays the canopy, partially obscuring the void.

I think we found the presence.

There's a ship out there. *Another* ship, and it's close. Like, really close, which isn't right. The shuttle's sensors are good, *really* good, because that's its primary function, to go out and scan stuff. Usually asteroids and moons and whatever the research teams find. It can find a rock small enough to fit in the palm of my hand from a thousand kilometres, and yet, it missed the hulk hanging in the dead of interstellar space. The thought of why that is doesn't bear dwelling on. If the fug can get to the shuttle, then this could be a one-way trip. I really don't want to be an alien meal.

I study the data on the screen. Really study it. Not simply the ship-shaped blob on the shuttle's sensors but the heat map. Whoever's out there, they're cold. Not in-the-lips-blue, but a frozen to the bone icicle. The shuttle is picking up the faint hum of power, but it's a thin shell, barely enough to make a blip on the sensors. Nowhere near enough to run life support or engines or an AI. Do aliens have AIs?

We're closer now, close enough for the shuttle to pick up more, things like carbon and the ship's age.

It's not fear that takes my breath, although that's there too, bottled up in my throat. It's awe. The ship was old before humans colonised Jørn. Which means this could be one of *Their* ships.

There's silence in my brain after that thought. Just... silence.

Wow.

If this is one of *their* ships, it's been here for a thousand years.

And there's something on it.

Alive.

Kinda.

Maybe in a coma, but it's breathing. I'm pretty sure, 'cause otherwise I wouldn't have sensed anything when I ventured in the place beyond the eter.

On the screen, the alien ship grows. Not that I can see it. It's still too far away for the visual sensors to pick up, but the shuttle AI does a good job of guessing.

A model of the ship appears in the middle of the console. It's not much at first, a barely formed blob of light swirling in the middle of the cockpit. After a few minutes of staring at an oval the size of my head, it starts to take shape. The oval flattens. Still round but thin in relation to its length, with a rounded bow and a sharp, almost fin-like stern, or what I guess is its stern.

It looks… it looks like *Citlali*.

That thought lodges in my brain and burrows deep, heading straight for the itch at the back of my brain where it's swallowed up like it never was.

The shuttle is mapping the ship's power now, lighting up the holo where it detects the greatest concentrations of energy, and since it's brightest at the sharp, fin-shaped bit, I'm guessing that's where the engines are. Assuming, you know, that aliens build ships like us (which apparently, they do) and use their engines to generate gravity.

I point the shuttle in the same direction the fug trail is heading, toward the broadest part of the bow, under where the curve starts to slope back to the stern. Can anyone say, "shuttle bay"?

I hope aliens can, otherwise I might have directed the shuttle into some kind of disintegrator or something. Or molecular destabiliser or hokey-pokey thing that's going to turn me into itty bitty chunks of frozen meat and bone.

I open up my brain and *reach* for the ship, ignoring the sense of stretching too far. I have to know why. Why they're here, why they're attacking us.

But there is no why. Nothing except that flat lifeless-but-not hum.

Whatever is on that ship, it's not aware enough to give me any answers.

✳

We dock.

There's a *THUNK* and a sharp jolt as the landing gear touches down. The fug continues to go around us. The floodlights cast stark shadows.

There's nothing in here. Nothing. If the... I guess I'm calling it a shuttle bay. If the shuttle bay had decking, it's gone now. As far as I can tell, the landing gear is resting on the struts between the superstructure, the beams where the plating should be. There are holes in the inner bulkheads, and I'm pretty sure I can see the leftovers of something that might have been a crane in the gaps. Everything in here is dead. Eaten. The only thing that appears untouched are the outer bulkheads and the airlock.

The place must have been huge when it was intact, twice the size of the Rec decks. There was space in here for a dozen of *Citlali's* shuttle bays. And now, with the decking gone and the holes, it seems bigger, like the inside of some giant skeleton. The shuttle's scanners are beeping and whirling, flooding the viewscreen with data. There's too much to look at, let alone take in and now that we're here...

I rub my nape, trying to ease an itch that won't go away.

I have to get out.

That thought comes out of nowhere, but I'm out of the flight chair and halfway across the cabin, making sure Dude's still in his pouch and reaching for my helmet before the train of thought finishes crossing my mind.

I shake my head.

No. No, that's not right.

I mean, I have to go out there, because why did I come all this way if I don't? But I have to do something else first. *Must* do something else first, I know I do I just...

The itch at the back of my head is making it hard to focus. I rub it and rub it, trying to push the fog out of my brain long enough to figure out what it is I need to do.

It's like trying to find my shoes first thing in the morning. I know I put them *right* there where I wouldn't forget them except sleep's still fogging my brain and that spot that seemed so logical last night is the most cryptic place in the universe. Damn it, why can't I remember?

I glance back at the viewscreen, at the skeleton of the shuttle bay, the fug floating past us, the blocks of *Citlali*, the heat and radiation signatures...

It hits me like a brick in the head, or maybe that's my palm connecting with my brow. Of course. Radiation.

'Shuttle, what's the outside atmosphere?'

'The immediate area is exposed to vacuum but scans suggest the inner structure has atmosphere. I am unable to analyse atmospheric makeup. Radiation levels are within acceptable limits. I would suggest full enviro protections until a more detailed analysis can be made.'

'Gravity?'

'None.'

Okay. So when I step out of the shuttle, I'm not going to die immediately.

The itch at the back of my brain settles as I turn toward the airlock, like it's happy that I'm headed in the right direction.

Which is weird, but there are other things to worry about.

Dude is tucked in his pouch against my chest, the helmet snicks into place over my head, the plasglas exploding into its dome as the airlock closes behind me. The hiss of air seems louder than usual, but it's only a second, and then the outer lock is cycling open and the ramp is extending.

There's no *THUNK* as it touches down. For one, sound requires atmosphere and two, the end of the ramp has missed the superstructure and is hanging out over the innards of the ship like a diving board. Good thing there's a whole heap of no gravity to go with the absence of atmosphere or I'd be taking a swan dive into the bowels of the ship. I step down the ramp far enough to clear the shuttle's tail, and then leap.

Zero gravity is kinda funky. It seems fun enough at first, floating and hanging out in weightlessness, but it's a real pain when you've got places to be and things to do. It's also not so easy to turn yourself around, and even though I aimed for the top of the shuttle bay when I took my leap, I must have fucked it up because I'm headed toward the bay's doors, the huge *open* doors with a really great view of the void beyond.

Shit.

Good thing EVA suits have thrusters.

A nudge to the spot inside my elbow activates the HUD on my faceplate and the suit controls blaze to life over the palm of my left hand. Like the shuttle, the suit's controls are little spheres only they're hovering over the tips of my fingers. It's the outer two I need, the ones over my thumb and little finger that control the thrusters attached to my back. I take a deep breath, trying to remember my last EVA training: Dad a pale dot hanging out in the void, barely visible to my eyes but lit up on the HUD, his voice in my comms.

'A gentle touch, Kuma. Like holding a critter. Too hard and you'll overshoot. Just take it slow.'

Just take it slow.

I hadn't of course, or at least, not slow enough. But I'm ignoring that bit, ignoring the memory of alarms screaming as I overshot Dad and went spinning into the dark.

'Okay, easy now,' I say to myself, holding on to the memory of Dad's voice. For a second, I think I sense him, the touch of his emotions, a warm golden glow that soothes my nerves.

A gentle touch.

I move my thumb.

The right thruster kicks in, humming against my back. I start to turn.

Thumb off.

The thruster cuts out. I keep turning, a little bit faster than before, but slow enough that there's time to get a good look at the void as it drifts past.

My heart's in my throat for those few, molasses-like seconds. Half awe, half fear. The memory of spinning into the void hisses and spits behind my eyeballs, the three hours I spent in space, alone except for the voices in my comms. Yeah. Good memories.

And then the bulkheads are cutting off the void and the HUD's scanning the bay, and I can shove the memory aside, concentrating on what comes next. There's a warm spot over my heart. Dude, *fuzzing* his shaven fur off. It helps, reminds me to take a deep breath and get ready for the next part.

There's a spot on the inner bulkhead, like a squashed egg lying on its side. I *think* it's a door. I aim for that.

Just before I'm facing the door, I hit the left thruster, a touch only. I stop spinning. Okay. Here's the hard bit.

Another breath. *Focus, Kuma. Focus.*

The HUD locks on the door, outlining it in bright green lines. More lines show up, outlining obstacles, distance, the fug. It's an obstacle course, up, down, sideways. A straight shot to the airlock would be best, but there's the trail of fug everywhere. It's parting around the shuttle like the vehicle is a stone in its pond, here's hoping it does the same for a lone Jørgen blitzing through its midst.

I hit both thrusters.

There's no jolt, no sense of movement, I'm being thrust across the bay like a mad rucnart. The shuttle disappears in the blink of an eye, the fug scatters, and the door is coming up too fast, getting bigger and bigger with every nano-second.

Too much, too much! I take my fingers off the thrusters but I'm still rocketing toward the bulkhead. For a second, my brain is blank. All I can think of is the metal rushing at my face and that this is going to hurt. Then my brains come back and a little voice says, not if I slow down.

That little bit takes over, rolling the control sphere above my index finger, steady even as adrenalin makes the rest of me shake. On my HUD, I see the thrusters swivel, and then, as the distance passes the double digits and into the single and the proximity alarm starts to blare, I hit the thrusters again.

It's like being jerked off your feet by the band of steelglas around your middle. My head and legs keep going even as my torso goes back. There's pressure on my chest, and a spurt of alarm as I imagine Dude getting squished in his pouch, and then it's over and I'm touching down on the lip of the airlock.

I take a moment to breathe. And then I take another to check on Dude, stretching my senses, searching until I find the fuzz of his thoughts. Brown stains the gold, a hint of discomfort but no pain, no fear, only the gentle golden glow and something different, not bad just... new.

But he's okay, and I let that be enough.

My heart settles.

So. I spread my hands over the door and activate my mag-boots. For a moment nothing happens and then there's a *thud* as I hit what's left of the deck-plating. How do I get past this?

The door is huge. Spreading my arms as far as they go doesn't even cover a fifth of it. Ten of me could stand like this, fingertip to fingertip and we might reach the other side. What was beyond it? What did *They* have to move that required shuttle access this big? They certainly didn't need it to walk through. If this was even one of *Their* ships. *They* didn't seem that big in the training memories, taller than a human, wider and bulkier, maybe the same size as a rucnart, if you ever got one to stand on its hind legs.

The back of my head itches, and I roll my shoulders, trying to ease the discomfort.

I gotta get through this door. But how?

The HUD's scanning the surface, but it's not really hooked up for detailed scans. I can see heat signatures and movement though, and there's a trace of power running through the bulkhead, a thin red-orange matrix. Most of the lines are too thin and too cold to see, but a few glow a thick, yellow-orange, hotter than the others, and they're all headed to the same place. I follow them, deactivating my boots and pushing off the door enough to propel myself in the direction of the energy stream. A few moments of floating through the vacuum and I'm hovering in front of something that *might* be a control pad.

The circle of... I don't know what it is. It's not made of the same, smooth, cold stuff as the door. There's power in it and some kind of curved, swirly ridges that look like a pattern but could be anything. I poke one of the smaller swirls. It's squishy, like biogel and I jerk my finger out before it sinks into the stuff. On the HUD there's a pulse of heat, faint but detectable, from the spot where my finger was. It runs through the pad and ricochets through the matrix within the door.

I wait. And wait. And wait some more.

I don't realise I'm holding my breath until my lungs start to burn.

The door opens. Not with a shudder or a slide or a cycle, but a snap, like a rubber band. I don't even see where it goes. One moment there's a huge slab of whatever is in front of my face and the next there isn't.

The air leaves my lungs in a rush.

Right.

Note to self, don't stand in the doorways.

A small hit on the thrusters and I'm scooting through the hatch.

The space on the other side is as huge as the door. Wide and tall, deep enough to fit *Citlali's* shuttle bay. I look up; except without the EVA vehicles hanging overhead. There's another huge door and another panel on the other side. I propel myself across the space. Parts of the decking here are intact and I'm able to land before the control pad without falling into the cavity below.

I stick my finger in the same small swirl. Power shoots outwards, and this time I remember to breathe and watch. There's a rumble behind me, and when I turn the door to the bay has snapped closed. I have a moment to panic, and then gravity takes hold. Literally.

I hit the deck hard, the shock running up from my soles, all the way through my shins to my teeth. It's not my mag boots, because my boots wouldn't make my head heavy. It's actual gravity. The

HUD's flashing data, something about oxygen and nitrogen, but there's no time to see it. I'm concentrating too hard on not falling over, into the hole behind me. I don't know how I managed to find the one spot with the shaft under it, but I've got a good view of the long, dark hole an inch from my feet. It didn't seem so scary when I was floating about in vacuum, but now? Yeah, gravity's a bitch.

The inner door snaps open as I'm losing my fight with it.

I leap.

I hit the opposite decking with my belly, hands scrabbling for purchase, legs kicking at the sides of the endless shaft. Somehow, one fingernail at a time, I slide out of the hole.

Is it me, or does this ship hate me?

My feet have cleared the doorway when it snaps closed, so close it scrapes the soles of my boots.

I roll onto my back. I'm going to lie here for a moment, remembering to breathe and admiring the ceiling while my heart slows and my body readjusts to not being dead.

The ceiling is really tall. And round, and intact. Mostly. There are few gaps in the... plating? I squint and my HUD enhances the image. It doesn't look like plating, at least not any that I've seen. It looks more like—

The HUD spits out data. Mineral analysis, depth, the ever-present heat map. The mineral analysis is weird, but then, I'm on an alien ship so what's *not* weird? Lying here, lying here is definitely weird. Not a great survival tactic, Kuma. What if one of *Them* comes... clomping (Strutting? Mincing?) down the hallway?

Yeah. Unlikely. Like five-hundred years unlikely.

I get up, and as I do, wonder why there's gravity. With the power so low and the engines off, it surprises me. But it's there, a little heavier than I'm used to. My screen is telling me it's one point zero four of Jøran gravity, not as heavy as some of the places I've been but enough to make it harder to lift my feet and make my muscles sore in the morning. I'm going to have to watch my oxygen use too. It'll be too easy to run the tank out with the slight increase; not so heavy as I'm going to feel it right away, but enough to make me breathe harder without realising. I set an alarm.

Two hours. That's how long I have to explore the ship, stop the fug and save Grea.

Yeah. Good luck to me.

At the moment, the only things in my favour are the ship's similarity to *Citlali* and the presence at the back of my skull. It's not the same as the itch at my nape, although that's still there too, making me wish I could take off my helmet. No, this presence is dragging me forward, guiding my feet like a lodestone. Following it is like muscle memory. Instinctual almost. And let's face it, with little else to go on, following it is better than wandering around an alien spacecraft trying to sort shit out.

The corridor outside the airlock heads off in two directions. I pick one and start walking.

CHAPTER SEVENTEEN

It's quiet, as quiet as the *Citlali* and yet not. I expect my steps to echo, to make the same *TANG TANG* as they do on the *Citlali's* decks, but the floor seems to swallow the sound. It's eerie.

The presence is somewhere ahead, a scent carried on the psychic breeze, sharp with the tang of copper and something else. Familiar in its unfamiliarity. Alien like Onah but not. Something about it reminds me of Ag, standing in there with a carpet of dead critters at her feet, staring at me like she's calculating my mass and water content, deciding on the best way to use my constituent parts.

It's unnerving, and I wonder what the fug is turning Ag into. Whatever it is, the presence grows with every metre I move down the corridor, the itch at my nape growing with it.

It's strange being here. As familiar/alien as the presence is, the ship is even more so. The corridor curves like the *Citlali's*, but where the *Citlali's* bulkheads have corners and crevices, sharp edges where wall meets ceiling, there's none of that here. There are no corners. The bulkhead is a continuous oval curve, if the oval was on its side and flattened on the bottom edge. There are no corners, not even where floor meets bulkhead, and the only sharp edges are the ones carved into the otherwise smooth walls.

I wonder what they are? Signs? Words? Pictograms? Or are they decoration?

I run my hands over them, tracing the curving lines and swirls. The carvings are shallow but the edges are sharp, my gloves catching on the ridges.

For some reason I imagine fingerprints carved into stone and now I'm wondering if ships can have fingerprints and why anyone, alien or not, would build a vessel out of stone. There's an Old Terran rabbit hole in that thought, and the urge to follow it is strong, a pulse that seems wrong.

I shake my head and step away from the bulkhead. It takes another few seconds to tear my eyes from the carvings. The whorls want to drag me into their centres and the lines want to drag me back to the whorls.

Pain spikes through my ear, jerking me out of the carving. Slapping the side my head is reflexive, but instead of the culprit all I hit is the side of my helmet.

A warm fuzz sneaks under my chin.

'Dude? Did you *bite* me?'

Dude fuzzes again and chitters in my brain.

'Well, thanks. I guess.' My eyes are drawn back to the walls. 'There's something strange about these carvings…' I don't realise I've stepped up to the bulkhead again, hand reaching out until another bright burst of pain shakes me loose.

'Holy Terra.' There's some really wrong shit going on with those carvings. *Really* wrong. 'Okay, Dude. New plan. Don't let me stare at the walls.'

Again, that chitter in my brain. Maybe I'm imaging it, maybe I'm not. Maybe the days isolated aboard *Citlali* and now in the heart of an alien ship have made me crackers, but it's better than being alone.

The alien ship *is* built like *Citlali*, the same concentric rings intersected by spokes running from a central hub. I guess that's how the fug knew to go for *Citlali's* core first.

The deeper I get into the ship, the more of it is familiar. Like a strange, grownup version of my home with a tattoo fetish. It's unsettling and I don't want to dwell on it too much. So far, I've studiously avoided it as I trek through the ship, going around and around for what might as well have been days but is just an hour. Every time I get close to the presence, I take another step and it seems to fade. It's taken me a few minutes to realise I'm on the wrong deck.

Turns out, aliens use stairs. Really big stairs.

My thighs ache from climbing the giant risers. The extra two percent of gravity makes all the difference. By the time I reach the top, my breath's coming in deep, ragged gasps from the pit of my lungs. The level on my oxygen pack has taken a nose-dive.

The stairs dump me on a deck like the last one. The presence is closer now, a buzz instead of a hum, pushing me forward while the itch at the nape of my neck rolls over my scalp.

The closer I get to the presence, the stronger the itch grows until it seems like it's in my bones.

I'm standing before a solid stretch of wall, indistinguishable from the rest. The presence is through there. I know it because if this were *Citlali*, this is where the door to Core would be.

That thought is disturbing.

I touch the wall.

Like the airlock, the wall shivers and a section wide enough for four of me to pass through becomes translucent before snapping open.

I don't want to step through. The picture of the thin membrane disappearing into the wall like a piece of freaky skin, is stuck in my brain. I can't quite help wondering what else around here is freaky skin-like. Am I going to run into consoles made of bone or workbenches made out of hair? Are there teeth in the cyclers? Oh my Terra, is the ship *alive*? Is the stuff following through its command circuits *blood*? What about the fug? What was that? Snot?

I shudder. Yuck. I had alien ship snot in my *mouth*.

I kinda want to heave, but that'd make a mess of my helmet so I roll the urge back down my throat.

A living ship would explain the presence. Never mind how much the idea makes my brain go gaga. It's possible, right? But still. Yuck.

I leap through the hatch, one of the doe-oc-like jumps that would have made Grea roll her eyes and stomp through after me to prove how much of wimp I was. The thought brings back the memory of Grea curled in tight ball in her pod, and makes my heart squeeze. I shove the memory back, because I know what comes after that and I'm not going to think about that, about the fug eating Grea's insides. Except I did and—

No. Just, no.

The hatch leads to another corridor, smaller than the main one, the curve of the walls steeper, but still wider than it is tall and I wonder again at the people who built it, and why it's so like *Citlali*. There's another hatch on my left, a few strides in, but it doesn't snap open at my approach. Instead the corridor continues, to another hatch nestled at the end. The presence is stronger now, a cold weight against my forehead, and it's pulling me toward the end hatch like a magnet. My feet move of their own accord.

I'm at the hatch without any memory of the steps between there and here, my hand on the strange skin-like material. It doesn't snap aside like the others, but it glows, like it's sucking the warmth from my hand. The glow spreads outwards, soft at first and then brighter and brighter. My faceplate polarises but I still have to close my eyes and even then, I can see the outline of my hand – a small shadow against the light of a sun. Then the light dies. I stare at the back of my eyelids a second before blinking them open.

It takes another second to dislodge the sunspots and for my eyes to focus, then another to figure out what I'm staring at.

The hatch is transparent, I can see the veins in it. Intricate, dark grey whorls and twists running around the edges of the skin, framing the room beyond.

It's like the rest of the ship, with curved bulkheads that merge with the deck, but unlike the rest of the ship it's round – a drop of water before it splashes on your nose. Unlike the rest of the ship, it's bursting with colour.

Purple and blue and lime and mawberry. So much colour it makes my eyes hurt. There's no rhyme or reason to it. It's a jungle, a really colourful, really bright jungle choked with vines and branches, around a single tree. I'm not sure how a single tree can make a jungle, but this does. In the centre of the room is a knotted trunk, off which everything grows. It's silver and shiny, with veins of mawberry and lime twining around it. I narrow my eyes and my HUD zooms in. The veins are pulsing; little muscles contracting and releasing, pushing light around the tree.

But it's not a tree. I know that like I know the atmosphere in the ship is a little too high in nitrogen and low on oxygen. Electro-magnetic waves pour off it, not strong enough to interfere with the HUD but enough to tell it's not sap running through those veins, but power. Enough power to stop my heart and start it again a million times over. But not enough to jumpstart an FTL engine.

I think I'm looking at the ship's AI. If aliens have AIs, I mean. What else could it be? And there's that presence. It's strong here, so strong that there's no doubt in my mind that this is where it's coming from.

I knock on the hatch. 'Hey. Computer?'

Silence answers me. I'm not really sure that I expected it to answer, I mean, why would an alien speak Jøran?

It was worth a shot, particular since the next step makes my heart pound with equal parts excitement and fear.

I open myself up to the presence, dragging it into my eter, the physical world dropping away. In the eter, the presence is smoke; grey and formless, static except for a faint shiver. It looks like the fug did when I first chased it through the eter, which means, if I focus on the shiver…

The smoke explodes.

There.

The shiver turns to reality-ripping lightning. I slide through one of the holes and—

Wow.

I didn't know those colours existed.

The psyche is exploding. What I thought was the dark, motionless lump of a comatose mind, was a shadow for the kaleidoscope taking up my vision. I can't describe it, but it's beautiful, as mesmerising as the bulkheads. I still can't sense any emotions or thoughts. It's like there's a plasglas wall between me and the presence. I can see it, but I can't sense it.

I press face and hands against the mental barrier, feeling my body doing the same against the hatch, and reach *around*. There's something, a croon against the sides of my mind, almost lost in the hum of my own thoughts. It's higher than I was expecting, like the AI is talking on a different bandwidth out of sight. Seeing it is like squinting while standing on my head, but once I do...

It's sleeping. The same death-sleep I noticed before, but there's more to it now, a tickle of hunger, a thrum of awareness, the sense of another there in the eter. I concentrate on that, pick at the threads, dragging it out of the sleeping mind until I recognise the creeping chill of the beacon.

There's more, a purpose and intent, but I can't touch it, can't follow it back to its source and unravel the mystery.

I need to get closer.

I return to my body and *emote*. There's no emotion for "let me in". The wave I push toward the trunk is a mixture of need and the bright, happy feeling of meeting old friends, of open doors and welcome.

For a moment there's no response. I'm gathering myself to *emote* again but... something's happening, a shift in the AI's colours. I wait, holding my breath.

SNAP and I'm catching myself before I fall through the now-open hatch.

A vine curls around the opening, a delicate pink tendril seeking my gloved hands.

I jerk back while Dude hums against my neck, except instead of menace rolling off his fur there's... *joy?*

'Dude?'

The little critter continues to hum, but louder, the vibration becoming a sound and the vine responds.

Re. Sponds.

Half of my brain is flipping out, while the other is saying, 'Well, shit.'

Of course, it's more of a shit-I'm-standing-on-the-threshold-of-an-alien-brain-and-my-critter-is-*talking*-to-it kind of shit than the regular kind of shit. It's also about the only thing holding me in place as I try to figure out how Dude's able to talk to fug, and how long he's been able to do it. The urge to run, to forget about reasoning with the AI and curling up in my stasis pod is strong, so strong my entire body vibrates with effort to resist.

At about the same moment the rational part of me gains the upper hand, the jungle parts. Fug slides across the deck, vines and tendrils retreat until there's a clear path to the trunk at its centre. A deep breath, and I step away from the hatch.

It *SNAPS* shut behind me.

My heart is pounding and I'm counting my breaths, not so much to slow them, but because I'll forget the need for oxygen otherwise. Dude's still humming, the warm happy gold of his presence butting up hard against the nerves running down my spine.

One foot in front of the other. Just. One foot in front of. The. Other.

I'm at the trunk before I have a chance to hyperventilate. Then I'm reaching out to touch it, ignoring the fug as it lifts and parts, forming a little tunnel big enough for my hand to fit through.

The trunk is firm. It undulates and wriggles against my palm, moving in and out like the lungs of some great beast while the fug writhes over my hand and up to my elbow.

It stops and squeezes, gently like the tendril at the door did, and again I get the sense it's shaking my hand… Or, rather, my forearm.

I grit my teeth and try not to flip out.

Dude's hum hasn't missed a beat.

I know it's nanotech, not snot or phlegm but microscopic bots controlled by the AI, but it still weirds me out. That doesn't matter now. I don't have *time* for it to matter.

The AI is right there, its presence a quiet hum against my palm. My eyes close of their own accord as I focus on the colours beyond my mind's eye. They're smooth, peaceful. I reach out, twisting my psyche a little to the right and upside-down and then I'm in.

Slipping into the AI is strange, but not like the maelstrom of before. It's just... different, a little uncomfortable, like doing the splits for the first time. My psionic muscles ache at the unfamiliar position. There's still a little ball of panic in my gut, but I'm able to hold it there, squish it before it blooms into something else. I can't afford any distractions, not this time. This time I have to do it right, whatever it is I'm doing. If it's even possible.

A deep breath and I plunge into the rainbow.

I'm a little Jørgen-coloured ball in the stream. For a second I'm caught in the current, the strange colours of the AI ripping at the thin shell of my shields. The panic slips my grip, exploding out from my middle in a puke-yellow wave. I catch it at the last second before it breaches my shields and spills into the stream. It takes another few heartbeats to bring it back under control, to stabilise myself in the stream and shore up my defences and then concentrate on navigating the swirls and eddies.

I stick to the main flow of the AI's mind, pushing away from the tributaries, from the whirlpools that want to suck me deeper. I've never seen a mind like this.

It's vast, complex, with different thoughts tugging at me from every direction. No, not thoughts – consciousnesses, fragments of the AI, split from the core like *Citlali's* sub AIs. Each of them demanding my attention.

Staying in the main flow takes all my concentration and yet...

Am I headed in the right direction? Does this mind even have a core? How much of it is AI and how much is... not?

The journey seems to go on forever and as the stream flows faster, the call of the other tributaries grows. One in particular is calling to me, a ribbon of bronze twisting in my skin, wrapping me in warmth and the promise of home. My concentration wavers—

The core explodes before me and I'm jolted back to my mission.

The AI shines with the brilliance of a faded star, not quite enough to blind me but bright enough to make it difficult to look at. This is it. The moment where I discover if I'm right or if I've fucked shit up. I *emote* a complex wave, the emotions shiny pink and green, the image of *Citlali* and safety riding on its crest. The stream ripples in its wake, the colours shifting. And then the wave hits the centre of it.

Everything stops. Right down to the molecule. I'm not sure how I can sense that, but I can. It's the only explanation for the fly caught in amber sensation that grips my entire being. Not just my psyche. Beyond the psionic plane my toes and fingers have frozen too, perhaps even the blood in my veins. The trunk is caught up in the freeze as well. The only thing that doesn't seem to stop is the fug. It contracts around my arm, turning hard, all the warmth draining out of it along with whatever colour it had, leaving a smooth grey sleeve. Cracks appear in it, fine lines running from my wrist all the way around the trunk, before the fug's smooth surface turns rough and powdery, the edges starting to crumble.

A pulse shoots through the AI, a surge of power that knocks me back, almost flinging me back into my body.

The core bursts to life. No longer glowing with the barely-watchable light of a fading star but the white-hot, socket-burning brilliance of a sun.

I made a mistake.

I'm in too deep.

Heat roars over me, a torrent of awareness pounding my shields. Of emotion and memory. Strange, incompressible tangles of colour that jar my eyeballs and snarl in my ears. It *hurts*, rips into my skull, grinds against my bones.

It's too bright, too alien. Too much.

I'm dissolving, turning to mush within the shelter of my own shields.

I close myself, huddle into a tight ball and concentrate on my skin, the way it wraps around bone and muscle, containing the thing that is me.

Kuma. A boy with golden skin and void-dark hair. Using my empathy to stop a fight and then start one. Running down a deserted corridor. Hands covered in the dust of a dozen broken pry bars. Burning fug. Saving Dude.

I am Kuma.

Aeotu. The thought slams into me, almost knocking me out of my new shell, an echo of my own name.

Aeotu. The name reverberated through the AI, saturating every particle, every strong colour and emotion, and I know, deep in the pit of myself, that it belongs to the AI.

My shields are dissolving, wearing away under the pressure of the AI's emotions. I hold them together as long as I can, but it's not enough.

The hunger slams into me first. A deep, gnawing sensation that eats at my bones and makes my skin hurt.

Behind the hunger there's something else, something that takes the panic in my gut and turns it to ice. I always thought fear was the worst emotion, but it's not. Loneliness is and it's got me in its grip. Spiky fingers digging into my heart, piercing the muscle and taking over my spine. I want to cry and scream and curl inside my stasis pod, clutching the memories of my family to me like Mum's hug.

It's not the loneliness I've felt the past days or weeks, one lightened by purpose and hope. It's deeper than that. Colder, deadlier, weighed down with centuries of hanging in the empty void of interstellar space. It's crushing me, squeezing me into a little ball of nothingness, except nothingness wouldn't hurt.

A familiar wave of emotion washes over me next, loosening the deadly chill of loneliness. Warmth gives me enough strength to uncurl, to reach for the promise of safety wrapped in the alien-but-not image of *Citlali*. Those are my own emotions, my own memory of home.

And I realise then, in that moment of emotion, that the *emote* worked.

Relief and joy wash over me. Those too are my emotions, but they're echoed by something stronger and bigger, something that doesn't match the ordered patterns of a mind built on logic. Something that's almost human, if humans were made of metal and nanites.

There's only one thing that it can be, and yet…

I can't quite twist my mind around it, can't quite grasp the significance. I try, honestly, I do, but it's so…

Sister. It's not a thought, it's more and less. An identification that slams into my gut and holds my heart hostage. It's me standing with my face pressed to the canopy of Grea's pod and the deep, instinctual knowledge that I'm going to get her out. It's hope and loneliness and love, and—

That's when it hits me.

Oh shit.

The Aeotu isn't an AI, it's alive. Not powered on and running at full capacity, but alive like *I'm* alive. Like a rucnart is alive. And it's got all the power of a hundred Regans.

I woke up a Regan *ship*. A sad, lonely, *hungry* ship. Really woke it up and told it that *Citlali* was home.

That takes another second to sink in. And in that second, through the veil of the eter, I feel the shudder as Aeotu's engines come to life.

Oh shit.

Ohshitohshitohshit.

We're screwed.

I rip myself out of the eter and away from the trunk, stumbling over roots and smacking into vines in my haste to get out of the core. Around me, everything has changed. The room is brighter, the walls pulsing and there's a hum now, almost too low to register. Not from the Aeotu's mind but something I can actually *hear*.

The engines.

I have to get back to *Citlali*. I don't know what I'm going to do when I get there, but I've got the whole shuttle ride back to figure it out. Somehow, someway I have to… I halt a few steps from the hatch and glance back at the trunk. What do I have to do? I don't even know what the newly awakened Aeotu is going to do, only that it sees *Citlali* as home and safe.

I reach back out to the AI, seeking it on the place beyond the eter. It's not hard. The hum in my ears is nothing to the vibration in my psyche – I can feel that in my chest, echoing through my ribs – and the colours are bright enough to blind my physical eyes.

Reading thoughts isn't something I'm good at. I can't actually reach out and grab them as most telepaths, or even Grea, can. I sort of open myself up like a big old net and hope they run into me. Organised thought has a sense, though, a vibration different from emotion. It's sharp and hard, an oval riding through the storm of emotion, coloured and tossed and changed, but always its own self.

There's nothing organised in Aeotu's mind, it's a confused, messy stream of consciousness. Only the *emote* shines strongly, that and the image of *Citlali*.

There has to be more. I dig deeper, spreading myself thin, riding the currents of emotion, ignoring the pain, the brightness that wants to turn me into a crisp. And there, behind the image of *Citlali*, behind the impression of home, is… is… I frown. It's an ugly, brown tangle of emotions, sparking with the red of anger, the black of fear and the brilliant white of intent. I reach for it, stretching myself a little thinner. The tangle is huge, as big as the ship itself, dwarfing me. I touch it with the tips of psionic fingers.

The scream rips out of my throat.

I'm back in my body, scooting backwards on hands and bum, gaze glued to the trunk, to the bright pulses shooting up and down it in shades of blue and yellow.

There's only one thought in my head, ringing over and over and over.

Protect. Images roll within the word, fragments. Giant tubes shooting out from her hull as she docked with Euvia, her sister ship. The aliens from the kins' memories scurrying out of Euiva, flooding Aeotu's corridors with the sick and dying as Euiva leaked atmosphere and her engines spluttered. The tubes disconnecting, the touch of Euiva's mind becoming fainter as Aeotu's engines fired, leaving her sister farther and farther behind, until she was nothing but a ghost on the sensors

Then the same events repeating, except it wasn't a sister this time, but Aeotu abandoned in the void, her crew gone. Limping through the black, repair nanites cannibalising systems. A hole in the hull. Bulkheads stripped. Gravity gone. And still, the inching coldness as the engines failed, and Sigrid still a distant star. Then, the last flicker of power and the endless cold.

Alone. But no longer. Euiva was out there. Euiva/*Citlali* back from the dead. Together they would go home. The image is burned on my mind, not just the outline of *Citlali* but what Aeotu intends to do. The ship moving, readying itself to grab hold of *Citlali*. The grapples, the giant docking bay. Not big enough to swallow *Citlali*, but enough to pull her close to Aeotu's hull, to initiate the link...

The link. Everything within me turns to ice.

I don't know what the link is, there were no details in Aeotu's thoughts, only the knowledge of what came next.

Faster-than-light travel.

I'm on my hands and knees, heading for the door before I have my feet under me.

What'd I do? What'd I do?

I have to get back to *Citlali*.

CHAPTER EIGHTEEN

The shuttle's landing gear has barely touched the deck before I'm out of the flight chair, blowing through the airlock and cycling the hatch open.

I'm down the ramp, halfway across the shuttle bay, Dude fuzzing against the back of my neck and my HUD screaming vacuum warnings, all of my attention focused on one thing.

Warn Core.

The control panel beside the inner door is a solid red. Locked. Of course it is.

A glance back over my shoulder, at the gapping rotten hole the fug has eaten in the bulkhead.

The inner bulkheads will be all that's stopping the last of *Citlali's* atmosphere shooting into space.

My brain is whirring, trying to recall *Citlali's* layout, the small maintenance tubes as I punch up my bio-computer. If I go back through the ice hull, I can find the aquifer that supplies Med and—

The inner doors open.

The gale of escaping air pushes me off my feet.

I scramble for purchase even as my mag boots activate and I steel myself to get blown into space.

And then it stops.

Citlali has more atmosphere than that. I glance up and into Core's floating gold face.

Her mouth doesn't move but her voice plays through my helmet's comms. 'Hurry, Kuma, the emergency airlock will not hold for long.'

Beyond her a sparkling blue energy field is strung between temporary pylons. I move.

The airlock is barely big enough for me and I can't help but suck my gut in as the bulkhead rolls closed. The energy field dissolves and I'm ripping off my helmet, turning to tell Core about Aeotu and *Citlali* and—

She's already halfway down the corridor, a disembodied head floating along in the wake of the drone. I stare at her for a second, mouth open.

'Hurry, Kuma.'

I hurry.

Dude's clinging to the neck of my envirosuit, fuzzing his fuzz off and I'm not merely hurrying, I'm jogging, boots *THUMPING* down the corridor.

'I need to tell you—'

'I know, Kuma.'

I stop. 'What?'

Core/drone disappears around a corner.

Shit. I run to catch up.

As soon as I'm in sight, Core starts talking. 'The fug stopped disassembling the ship. It now appears to be repairing it.'

Confusion slows my steps; Core continuing hastens them again. 'Outer hull breaches and structural deformities are being repaired, but sensors have detected several abnormalities.'

'Your sensors are working?'

'Yes, Kuma. The new critters are proving effective against the fug and I have been able to restore several systems, including drone control.'

Grea. 'Stasis?' Hope lifts my heart even as exertion makes it pound.

'Not yet.'

And there it goes, crushed under the weight of fug. I stop dead, hands on my knees as I drag in air.

Core/drone appears in my line of sight.

'Kuma, we must hurr—'

'Aeotu's going to swallow *Citlali*.'

It's Core's turn to look like a stunned qwan, mouth gaping open.

'Aeotu's the source of the fug. It believes *Citlali* is its sister ship and it's coming to take us home.' I pause. '*Its* home.'

Core's frozen, mouth still open.

Three heartbeats. Four. Six. Ten.

This is more than the pause when she's trying to process telepathic impossibilities.

My breathing's back under control, sweat cooling on my forehead. I straighten.

Core's still frozen, but now there's cubes of static shivering through her head.

Alarm blooms in my chest.

'Core? Core!'

What if the fug got her? She said it was modifying things, what if—

A blink and Core/drone zips to eye level.

'Aeotu has appeared on short range sensors. I've analysed the modifications the fug is making and the other ship's trajectory. It would appear you are correct. Come with me.'

Core/drone led me to Engineering.

Main engineering, where Jim Engineer pulls shuttles and workbees apart, is at the top of the ship – only the Atrium, a tiny pocket wedged in the ice hull, is above it – but there are small engineering sections on every deck, running the stern of the ship.

The section Core/drone takes me to is one of those. A small, cramped space that resembles a closet more than a workspace.

There's fug damage all over the place, holes in the bulkheads, the benches, the floor. A whole section at the back is gone, opening onto a maintenance tunnel, and beyond that a freight tube and beyond that—

I swallow and point through the fug-eaten ship to the almost-dead miniature sun beyond. 'Are those the engines?'

'Yes.'

'There's a hole in the plating,' are the words that come out of my mouth, but what I'm really wondering is how soon the engines are going to come on and fry my brain.

'Emergency shielding continues to function. Kuma Darzi, I need you to focus here.'

A light shoots from the drone, highlights another fug-eaten bulkhead, this one more like Mac's favourite swiss cheese than steelcrete. Through the hole, platform gleams; snitches of red and vibrant blue, interspersed with white.

A storage unit. The wall pops out, fragile bits of decayed steelcrete crumbling with the sudden movement.

The gleaming colours and shapes are tools, three solid rounded bodies the length of my forearm, surrounded by a wall of silver attachments.

'What am I meant to do with this?'

Core/drone hovers at my side. 'You're going to make a Franken-laser.'

CHAPTER NINETEEN

The ship shudders, a violent heave that lifts me off my feet and throws me into the wall. Ahead of me, Core/drone barely avoids careening into the bulkhead, her stabilisers firing a moment before her plasform shell smashes into the steelcrete.

'What was that?'

'I do not know, Kuma, exterior sensors are still offline.'

'Can't you guess?'

'That is not within my programming, however...' She's silent a moment as she rights herself and continues bobbing along the corridor. I rush after her. 'Interior sensors are picking up a change in atmosphere not in line with *Citlali's* usual operation.'

'And that means?'

'We have been boarded, Kuma.' Core's avatar appears in the corridor in front of me, the drone passing through her head like it wasn't there. 'We are now attached to the *Aeotu*.'

I run faster, Core splintering around me as I sprint through her avatar.

I have to get to the Atrium.

'Interior sensors are showing an influx of fug.' Core keeps pace with me, her avatar now bobbing along behind the drone. 'It appears to be concentrated around the grappling lines. I cannot determine what it is doing.'

The new Franken-laser bounces against my back. There's no air to talk. Oxygen is burning up in my lungs, my heart pumping it out to my muscles, every step vibrating up my shins, through my knees with the thought 'Go.'

The freight shaft is there, the hatch a patchwork of holes and critter fuzz. I'm through it, ready to run again, when Core/drone flashes red and stops.

I skid to a halt, nose millimetres from her shell.

'What—?'

The *WHOOSH* of rushing air and the bright pulse of the mag lines stops me. I turn.

The sled is on us before I can blink.

There's time enough to jump, a blind leap that throws me against the crumbling tunnel wall before the sled shudders to a halt where my knees used to be.

'Climb on, Kuma.' Core/drone hovers over my head.

'What?' I'm still staring at the sled, imagining it ploughing into my knees.

'The sled. Get on.'

'Oh.' I swallow. 'Right.'

No sooner am I on the sled, it takes off. There are no wind shields on a freight sled, nothing to cut the howling gale that screams past my ears or the pressure that brings tears to my eyes. There also doesn't appear to be any speed control, because I'm plastered against the thin lip that runs all the way around the sled, unable to move. Soon enough I'm forced to close my eyes against the pressure, and then I'm struggling to lift my arm, to turn my head to escape the pressure of the blasting wind against my lids. I can't tell if we're going up or down, and Core must have turned the gravity off, because the Atrium is at the top of the ship and surely, we have to go up.

I hope we get there soon, because it's getting hard to breathe now, hard to hear my heart past the rush of air.

And then the pressure lets up, my lungs no longer fighting the press of my ribs, and I can move my arm.

The sled stops.

I tumble off. Stars bursting in my vision.

I should name them, I mean, I've seen them often enough, and the Kuma Hit His Head constellation has a nice ring to it. Grea will laugh.

Core/drone is already darting forward, through the door before I finish blinking the lights from my eyes.

I stumble to my feet, the Franken bouncing against my back.

There's no corridor beyond. We've reached the Atrium, *Citlali's* top deck, a huge open space to rival the three Ag decks, and the only place on the ship with an actual view of the void. Except now, instead of a million pinpricks of light, all I see is the sleek lines of Aeotu's hull.

'Vacuum!'

Vacuum, the warning cry that parents yell in the night instead of "fire". My hands are moving, a lifetime of midnight drills taking over, activating my helmet before the rest of me catches up.

And that's when I see the crack in the hull.

A giant cable has pierced the steelcrete and plasteel, punching a hole all the way through the hull and into the deck. The steelcrete is deformed inwards, the deck the same. The bright blue of an emergency shield plays in the space around the shattered hull, sparking white around the invading cable as it tries to stop our atmosphere from escaping into the nothing of space.

Behind me, more bulkheads snap closed, protecting the rest of the ship and leaving me alone with Core/drone and Aeotu.

I swing the Franken around, holding it with both hands.

The grappling cable is thicker than a shuttle, a giant silver-black column in the middle of the Atrium. I heft the Franken, my finger on the trigger, and stalk toward it.

It gets bigger, seeming to grow in size in the two dozen steps it takes me to reach the edge of the rip it's made in the deck. I ignore the doubt in my gut, the whisper asking if the Franken will even scratch its surface, and press the trigger. Light blazes, a thin, focused beam that cuts through the air and slices into the cable.

And for a moment I have hope. Watching it slice into the metal, the beam slicing into the silver-black, a centimetre gone with every beat of my heart, and another and another. This might work. This might actually work!

There is something under the silver-black, a glimpse of red like blood, squeezing and pulsing and—

The scream knocks me off my feet.

It rings in my head, louder than anything, than the fug, than the *Citlali*'s engines than, than...

My bones are vibrating, my skull exploding, my ears...

The sound's not in my ears. My hands are on my helmet, gripping the plasform like they can squeeze the sound out of my head, and the HUD's flashing, all systems normal. I see that, somehow, through the pain. The scream is in my head, it's psionic, carried on the multicoloured, fractured light of Aeotu.

Core/drone is bobbing in front of my face, and I know she's trying to tell me something, can hear the words, actual words, through the scream in my head but they don't make sense. I can't... I can't—

The world goes black.

I'm in the Atrium, staring up through the plasteel roof, the thin bubble that punches through the ice hull, except that instead of stars, I'm seeing intricate shadows, whorls and lines shifting under yellow lights. Those aren't the shields that normally protect the Atrium and I wonder at that a minute, and why the sight of it makes my gut cramp and cold slither through my bones.

And then I remember.

'Shit.'

I'm rolling to my feet, or trying. My head swims, and getting to my knees is enough to make me stagger, to fall forward on my hands. Dizziness swamps my vision, and for a second I'm staring at the deck, trying to remember what I'm doing. There's something pulling at my chest and shoulder. I reach for it, touch the strap and I remember. This time I make it to my feet, using the Franken as a crutch.

The grappling cable's still there, an ugly scar through it but now it's pulsing. The *scar* is pulsing, not simply with movement but with colour. So many colours I can't name them all.

I hobble closer, lifting the Franken, finger on the ignition and… stop.

The pulse is changing. No longer the rhythmic *thump thump thump* of a heart but a flutter, a *th-th-th-th* pause *THUMP*.

Th-th-th-th.

Pause.

THUMP.

Th-th-th-th.

Pause.

There's something in there. In the pause. It's staring at me from the maelstrom of colour, reaching into my anima and pulling me toward it.

I know you. Know that storm, the lightning, the vast, complicated pathways. The socket-melting brilliance of its core.

'Aeotu.' The name is a whisper, trapped within the confines of my helmet and vacuum, and yet…

And yet the pause *smiles*.

Beckoning. Beckoning.

SISTER.

I'd leap a kilometre if I could, but a kilometre wouldn't be far enough. 'Holy Terra.'

That voice, that voice came through my *comms*.

My. Comms.

But how?

'Core? Core!'

Static, a golden face that flickers and spits on my HUD.

'Core? What's happening? Aeotu's hacked my comms.'

'Evacuate, Kuma Darzi. All systems compromised. Stasis separation initialised.'

Stasis separation.
Every microjoule of warmth leaves my body.
Run.

CHAPTER TWENTY

I run until my lungs ache. I run until I taste blood and there's not enough oxygen left in my suit to take a full breath. I run until my legs are jelly and spots fill the edge of my vision.

I run and I run and I run.

Emergency bulkheads open before me and snap shut on my heels. I stop only when the map on the HUD tells me. All the while trying to get Core's not-voice out of my head.

Stasis separation.

It echoes through my bones, burrowing deeper with every jarring stride. The speedway's up ahead, a waiting palette illuminated in the spitting lights. I jump on. It takes off.

Stasis separation.

The grappling cable took out the section of speedway I'd arrived on, obliterated it like the steelcrete were Old Terran paper, or tissue or skin... or... or....

Stasis separation.

I run and jump and tumble down maintenance ladders half-eaten by fug, all the very long way to Lab One, at first following Core's voice and then the map after the AI froze on my HUD, brows raised and her eyes wide in an expression of surprise real enough to send bolts of alarm through my gut.

Only two more decks to go and I was on Stasis.

There's another voice at the back of my head, knocking on my skull, trying to worm its way into my marrow.

Sister.

No. I push it away, wall up my psyche and concentrate on the rush of lights and shadow, the hum of the palette on the mag lines. Concentrate on the cold, hard lump of fear behind my heart and try to convince myself that it's going to be okay, that we're not going to be lost in the void. Like Aeotu.

Sister.

The palette slams to a stop, throwing me across the slab of steelcrete and against the guard rail at the front. I have time to gasp, to grab a new handhold before we plummet. It's seconds but it seems like hours that I'm flying through the air, feet over my head, hands cramping around the guard rail, sweat slicking the inside of my gloves, muscles screaming as gravity tries to rip my arms from their sockets.

Then more pain, new pain, slamming into the palette, curling in on myself at the last second, my shoulder crunching against steelcrete, fire consuming my back, my arm, my fingers, even as I flail for the rail, only one hand working.

I've barely got a finger on it before the palette roars sideways.

I'm slammed into another guard rail, and now that fist in my back is a dagger in my chest and an alarm screaming on my HUD.

But there's no time. No time.

Only three words float through my brain, each one worse than the last.

Stasis.

Separation.

Sister.

A final shuddering halt, as bone jarring as the last. I want to curl into a ball, but those three words keep me going.

The map flashes on my HUD, almost hidden under the med warnings.

The speedway has dumped me on Med/Command, at a small freight dock. One more deck to Stasis. One more deck. I can do that. I slide off the palette, stumble to the controls and try to ignore the dagger digging into my chest with every breath.

The door opens. There's a drone waiting for me, hovering at head height, Core's gold face projected before it.

'Core?'

Nothing. The AI is frozen.

I shuffle forward, reach out, gloved fingers passing through Core's nose.

The holo shudders, begins to speak and I know from the way her gaze skims over my head, that it's a recording. If Core had been there, she'd have looked me in the eye.

'Kuma, separation systems compromised. Manual engagement required. Instructions in drone.'

The drone leads me to a hole in the deck. A literal hole, the edges ragged and crumbling, fug clinging to the steelcrete. Most of the fug is inert, the once grey-green strands now just a dull grey, but some of it still moves, and its colour has changed as well, to a bright red that makes something deep down in the pit of my being want to scream and hide.

I swallow. Core said the fug was repairing the *Citlali* now, not eating it, and there are more important things to worry about.

Power sparks in the thick section of deck and shimmers in the waterfall of biogel from broken conduits. Beyond is Stasis.

I can't see it, but I know it's there. Unless the fug ate through the floor below.

The drone hovers over the hole.

'Down.' It uses Core's voice and face, but it's not Core, its tone flat, its expression wooden. 'Down,' it says again, the face morphing into an arrow plunging into the darkness.

Just in case I didn't know where down was, I guess.

'Gravity's still on.' Jumping down that hole's going to hurt.

'Down.' The drone hovers closer. 'Down.'

The fact that falling a few metres in full gravity is going to break more of my bones doesn't seem to bother it.

Okay. I grab the drone, hugging it to my chest, step off the deck and let gravity take hold. Pain slams through my chest as the drone's antigravs whine and the thing shakes, throwing itself left and right and into my ribs.

I grit my teeth and hold tighter.

The drone thrashes, my grip loosens, slips and—

The deck slams into my feet, not hard enough to break bones but enough to force a groan from my lips as the vibration ricochets through my ribs.

My vision blurs, or maybe that's the drone darting out of reach.

I take a moment to push the pain aside then I'm on my feet and following the drone again. Pain swamps my side, turns my pace into a shuffle, narrows my vision.

'How much farther?' My voice is hoarse, the words difficult to get out.

The drone doesn't answer.

I want to stop, to catch a breath that's suddenly coming too short, but I have to keep going, have to keep going.

Something skittles up my leg.

I yell, jump sideways and try to keep my feet as pain balloons, swamps my vision, takes my breath.

A golden fuzz shivers through my shoulder, dulls the pain.

Breathing comes easier, my vision clears.

'Dude.'

He chitters, the not-sound warming my skin, chasing away the fear that's been with me since the Atrium.

The drone flashes, lighting up the hallway, and in that brief flash I can't ignore the holes, the pockmarks and cracks that lace the bulkheads. There's fug there too, most of it dull and grey but some, some of it writhes in between the breaches in thick pulsing webs of blood, almost as if it's trying to stitch the damaged steelcrete together.

Maybe it's a trick of the shadows, or the pain gnawing at my chest, but for a moment I swear it's watching me, those red strands reaching out, whispering in my ear.

Sister.

I yank my mind away, close it off, wall it up and think of something, anything else.

It's not hard.

I need to get to the separation controls, need to save the crew, save Grea, and yet…

My eyes snag on the bulkheads, the holes in the steelcrete. Through them my HUD picks out the hum of stasis pods, the pulse of blood in veins. If Stasis separates, those people will only have the thin skin of emergency shields to protect them, and when the power dies, so will they.

'Core. Core, we can't do this. The units are compromised.'

Static on the comms and the drone shooting ahead of me.

I hobble after it, ignoring the dagger stabbing me in the side with every shuffle, concentrating only on the drone and the new, desperate knowledge that I need to stop this, to warn Core. It's almost enough to block the whisper at the back of my skull.

I don't know where the drone's leading me. The emergency separation controls are at the centre of the deck, two rings out from Core, and we're heading outwards. Maybe the fug ate those controls, maybe there are secondary ones in the outer rings. Maybe Core saw the damage and is… is what? Getting me to repair the bulkheads before the alien ship swallows us whole?

Come on, Kuma, you're not that stupid. There are no secondary controls. Even you know that. So why the lie?

The drone's stopped in front of a stasis unit. There's no name on the hatch, only a number and the tag "SOS" stencilled in orange. It opens and inside it's like all the other units, four stasis pods side-by-side, the unmissable "EMERGENCY SUPPLIES" on the rear bulkhead, except the pods are empty.

I'm back-peddling as fast as the pain in my chest will let me, 'cause I know what's happening now, know Core lied because otherwise,

otherwise I would have... What? Fought an alien spaceship? Grabbed a multitool and started welding bulkheads while my ribs slowly punched a hole in my lung? Would have saved the day with nothing but my bare hands and a faithful critter at my side?

My breath's coming hard, fogging up the HUD and my heart's pounding.

No. No. It doesn't end like this.

The drone flickers and now it's wearing a hasty copy of Core's face, its expression wooden, eyes staring somewhere over my shoulder.

'All stasis units compromised. Unable to complete full separation.'

And now I'm hobbling forward, making up all the distance I put between us. 'We can fix it. I can get a repair kit and the critters—'

'Engine containment has been breached. Emergency shielding will fail.'

Engine containment. My mind flickers back to the miniature sun glimpsed through a hole in Engineering. Picture the blue energy field around it growing dim then dying. I don't *know* what happens next but I can imagine it, a wave of light and heat turning my atoms to dust.

The holo shudders and suddenly it's *Core* staring at me, the lines of her face shifting, turning the concern and urgency of her expression into something that's almost real, as the AI takes over from the hasty fragment left in the drone's circuits.

I lunge toward her. There's a thought worming its way to the forefront of my head, an idea that if I can grab her, touch her, I can reach through the drone and make the AI *understand*.

Understand what, I don't know. It's a fuzzy, urgent, terrified emotion permeating every fibre of my being. But I know, *know* I can save us, if only—

Core/drone zips out of reach and I have to catch myself on the open hatch before I fall through it.

I turn.

And that's when the fug pounces.

Dude leaps from my shoulder, fangs and tiny claws bared, a split-second before the drone slams into my chest.

I'm flying backwards, heel catching on the stasis unit's seal as Dude meets the red fug head-on.

And then the air's exploding out of my chest and the drone's shooting back up, arrowing for the hatch.

Urgency helps refill my lungs, fight past the pain and panic, roll to my feet.

The hatch is closing.

The drone's on the other side, probes in the control panel, and there's Core's voice. 'Stasis separation in fifteen seconds.'

'What? Wait. No!'

'Goodbye, Kuma.'

'No. Dude!'

The hatch closes.

I slam into it, already scrambling for the controls. No. No. No. I wasn't leaving him to the vacuum.

The control pad dies. Just. Dies.

Okay. Don't panic. The emergency lever—

CLUNK.

The sound reverberates through the bulkhead, everything in me stills. No. Not yet.

SHUSSSH.

That one's barely even a sound, it's a feeling, a sensation shivering up my spine, swallowing me in dread.

'No.' I'm on my knees, pushing the emergency panel out. There's still time, there *has* to be time. The panel comes away and there's the lever and—

SSNUCK.

The lever's gone, sucked into the hatch at the same time the stasis unit shudders, the gravity goes and—

"DANGER. VACUUM."

The words are too big to miss, letters as big as my head popping into existence over the door.

I punch the hatch, kick it, slam my hands into the steelcrete but…

nothing. Even the biogel feels dead. Hard. Cold.

No. No no no no no.

I grab hold of the panel, pound on the door and try to ignore the fact that I'm floating half a metre off the deck.

'Core! Open up! Core!'

The power goes, the holos and lights with it.

I scream, the sound echoing in my helmet, high and sharp, matching the pain in my chest. The fire of the rib pressing on my lung, mixing with the claws wrenching my heart in two, shredding the muscle, ripping it apart until there's nothing left but me.

Just me.

Alone in the dark...

...Sister.

THE ADVENTURE CONTINUES IN

DARK BETWEEN OCEANS

THE ECHO 2

Scan the QR code or visit the link below to get it now.
belindacrawford.com/DarkBetweenOceans

DO YOU WANT MORE?

I love keeping in touch with my readers, it's the second-best thing about being a writer (writing being the first best). Every fortnight (or thereabouts), I send out a newsletter with details about upcoming offers, new releases and extra special projects.

If you sign up for the mailing you'll receive exclusive behind-the-scenes extras, such as:

- free short stories
- deleted and alternate scenes from The Echo
- previews of my upcoming books
- pancakes
- quizes
- and much, much more!

Scan the QR code or visit the link below to sign up.
belindacrawford.com/newsletter

ACKNOWLEDGMENTS

Writing and publishing a book is a lot like packing up a house; you write and you write and you edit and you format, and you think you're almost done, and then you remember the Acknowledgments.

The worst bit about acknowledgements is trying not to write the same thing you did last time. I mean, there are only so many ways you can say 'it takes a lot of people to publish a book, and I would like to thank...'. That's what they're all about, after all, saying thank you to the people who:

- put up with you storming around the kitchen when you don't know what to write next (thanks Mum)
- listen to you rabbit on, yet again, about how you have no idea how to get Kuma to the Med deck (thanks Tracy)
- read the manuscript and pick up all the niggly plot holes before it goes to the editor (thanks Tracy, Iffet and Roger)
- edit the damn thing (thanks Amanda J Spedding)
- inspired you to try writing a novel without plotting it first (this one's all you Devin Madson).

And then there are the Kickstarter Heroes, a small group of people who supported the special edition of *Cold Between Stars** before it was even finished. These Heroes have a special place in my heart because they make many wonderful things (like special illustrated editions) possible, they are: Amelia Soon, Iffet, Gaby van Halteren and Ruth Molenaar. Thanks guys, you're legends.

*Yes, there's a special edition, it has illustrations and if it's not already in your hot little hands, check it out on my website.

ABOUT THE AUTHOR

Physics makes Belinda's brain hurt, while quadratics cause her eyes to cross and any mention of probability equations will have her running for the door. Nonetheless, she loves watching documentaries about the natural world, biology, space, history and technology.

She's also a sucker for a fast horse, a faster computer and superhero movies. When she's not doing the horse, computer or superhero thing, Belinda writes science fiction (emphasis on the fiction), where she loves to write about butt-kicking girls (and guys!) who blow stuff up.

You can keep in touch with Belinda, or just pick her brains about sci-fi via her website, Facebook or by sending her an email (she loves email).

www.belindacrawford.com
belinda@belindacrawford.com

Have news delivered straight to your inbox
via her mailing list. Sign up at:
belindacrawford.com/newsletter

www.ingramcontent.com/pod-product-compliance
Lightning Source LLC
Chambersburg PA
CBHW030427120726
47903CB00003B/846